JB 5/16

SPECIAL MESSAGE TO READERS

This book is published under the auspices of

THE ULVERSCROFT FOUNDATION

(registered charity No. 264873 UK)

Established in 1972 to provide funds for research, diagnosis and treatment of eye diseases. Examples of contributions made are: —

A Children's Assessment Unit at Moorfield's Hospital, London.

•

Twin operating theatres at the Western Ophthalmic Hospital, London.

•

A Chair of Ophthalmology at the Royal Australian College of Ophthalmologists.

•

The Ulverscroft Children's Eye Unit at the Great Ormond Street Hospital For Sick Children, London.

You can help further the work of the Foundation by making a donation or leaving a legacy. Every contribution, no matter how small, is received with gratitude. Please write for details to:

THE ULVERSCROFT FOUNDATION,
The Green, Bradgate Road, Anstey,
Leicester LE7 7FU, England.
Telephone: (0116) 236 4325

In Australia write to:
THE ULVERSCROFT FOUNDATION,
c/o The Royal Australian and New Zealand College of Ophthalmologists,
94-98 Chalmers Street, Surry Hills,
N.S.W. 2010, Australia

Neil Cross is the author of several novels, including *Burial.* He is the creator of the new BBC crime series *Luther* and was previously lead scriptwriter for the acclaimed spy drama series *Spooks*. He lives with his wife and two children and continues to write widely for the screen.

CAPTURED

Although he is still young, Kenny has just weeks to live. Before he dies, he wants to find his childhood best friend Callie Barton and thank her for the kindness she showed him when they were at school together. But when Kenny begins his search, he discovers that Callie Barton has gone missing. Although her husband Jonathan was cleared of any involvement, he seems to be hiding something. Kenny has no choice but to take matters into his own hands. And knowing that time is running out on him, he's prepared to do whatever it takes . . .

Books by Neil Cross
Published by The House of Ulverscroft:

BURIAL

NEIL CROSS

CAPTURED

Complete and Unabridged

ULVERSCROFT
Leicester

First published in Great Britain in 2010 by
Simon & Schuster UK Ltd., London

First Large Print Edition
published 2010
by arrangement with
Simon & Schuster UK Ltd., London

British Library CIP Data

Cross, Neil.
Captured.
1. Terminally ill- -Fiction. 2. Abused wives- -Fiction.
3. Suspense fiction. 4. Large type books.
I. Title
823.9′2–dc22

ISBN 978–1–44480–327–3

Published by
F. A. Thorpe (Publishing)
Anstey, Leicestershire

Set by Words & Graphics Ltd.
Anstey, Leicestershire
Printed and bound in Great Britain by
T. J. International Ltd., Padstow, Cornwall

This book is printed on acid-free paper

To Gordon and Michael

To Francesca

And to Nadya, Ethan and Finn — always

1

Kenny wrote the list because he was dying.

Earlier that morning, an MRI scan had revealed that a malignant brain cancer had germinated in the moist secrecy of his skull like a mushroom in compost.

He had six weeks, maybe less. Aggressive chemotherapy and a brutal, invasive procedure called a partial resection might extend that by a month. But Kenny didn't see the point.

So he thanked his doctors, left the hospital and went for a walk.

* * *

It was mid July, and the humid afternoon was beginning to cool. The pavement smelled of rain evaporating from hot concrete.

On Castle Green, Kenny sat down. He wore cargo shorts and a T-shirt. He had a head of dandelion white hair. He watched the office workers and the cars and the buses and the taxis. Then he called Mary.

She answered on the second ring, a cheery: 'Hiya.'

'Hiya.'
'You okay?'
'Yeah!'
'You don't sound it.'
Years before, Kenny and Mary had been married. They weren't married any more, but you never stop knowing someone's voice.
Kenny said, 'So — you fancy meeting up?'
'I can't tonight, love. I've got stuff.'
'For five minutes? A sandwich.'
'Oh, look. By the time I get down there . . . Tomorrow, maybe?'
'I can't tomorrow. I've got a client.'
'The day after, then. Thursday? Are you okay?'
'I'm great, yeah. I'm good.'
'Really?'
'Really.'
'So let's do Thursday, then. Picnic lunch if it's sunny?'
'That sounds good. I'll give you a call.'
He said goodbye, hung up and put the phone in his pocket.
He made sure he had his house keys and his wallet. He went to pick up the prescription of anticonvulsants and corticosteroids that would make his next few weeks a bit more comfortable.
Then he strolled to the bus-stop. It wasn't far, and he was in no hurry.

2

The village was outside Bristol, on the North Somerset Levels. It took the bus a while to get there, but Kenny didn't mind.

Sometimes, when he had a lot to think about, he took the bus. It relaxed him. And he liked taking the bus; he liked the way it jerked and jolted, picked up passengers, set them down. He liked the way people called out 'Cheers, driver!' as they alighted.

When the bus reached his stop, Kenny disembarked.

The village was old, houses raised from stone the colour of shortbread. There was a church which dated to the Norman Conquest. A scattering of commuter new-builds stood on the outskirts.

Kenny lived in what had been a gamekeeper's cottage. You walked half a mile outside the village, turned off the main road, down a bumpy lane with trees either side and grass growing in the middle, and there it was.

It had been remodelled and extended many times. The last refit, sometime in the 1950s, had added an indoor bathroom.

Outside the cottage stood many corrugated

outbuildings and the rusting carcasses of Morris Minors — they'd been there when Kenny bought the place, a decade before.

Brambly hedges and a mad overgrowth of rhododendrons edged a fast-flowing brook. Across all this, Kenny had a fine view of dairy farmland and the motorway, heading east towards the Cotswolds and west towards Wales.

He lived in the largest and brightest room, arranging it like a studio flat, with a bed and a wardrobe and armchairs and bookcases and a television.

This room gave him direct access to the kitchen. Beyond the kitchen a long corridor gave on to a number of cold, damp bedrooms which Kenny never used. It also gave on to the large conservatory he used as a studio.

Even on overcast days, the conservatory had a good light. It was full of easels, half-completed paintings, sketches, paints, brushes, rags, jam jars.

Kenny had a talent for faces. It made him a pretty good portrait artist.

He'd tried other things; for a few years he'd worked as a designer for a little advertising agency on the Gloucester Road, designing logos for local firms. He illustrated promotional brochures, did some work for the town council.

But these days, he just did portraits.

* * *

He sat there, in his favourite chair, and he thought for a while. Then he went to find a notepad and thought for a while longer, chewing the end of his pen, before writing:

Mary
Mr Jeganathan
Thomas Kintry
Callie Barton

It was a list of people he'd in some way let down. He'd decided to use the time he had left to put things right.

3

Mary was sitting on the grass in Brandon Hill Park, with Bristol spread out below her. She was reading a book, waiting for him.

As Kenny approached — a rucksack slung across one shoulder and a carrier bag in his hand — she smiled a big smile, her Kenny smile.

Lowering himself to the grass, Kenny said: 'You're looking lovely.'

She waved a hand, pretending to blush.

He opened the bag, passing her a small bottle of freshly squeezed orange juice and a fruit salad in a plastic pot. She passed him a BLT. They sat eating for a bit, throwing sandwich crusts to the greedy squirrels. Then Kenny said: 'So how's it going?'

'Gangbusters. You?'

'Not too bad. I've been doing some thinking, though.'

'About what?'

'Nothing really. Just stuff.'

'Stuff like what?'

'Like, are you happy?'

'Oh, stuff like that.' She frowned at him — it was a silent question. 'I'm happy, yeah.

The kids make me happy. Stever's an arsehole.'

Stever was a kind man, and Mary loved him. She and Stever had been married for five years.

Kenny was godfather to their children. He loved the kids — he liked to scream and roll on the floor and join in. He liked to read them bedtime stories, doing all the voices. He liked to draw pictures for them, too — Transformers and ballerinas, cats and dogs and Jedis and monsters made of dripping bogies.

He nodded, now, thinking of it, and unzipped the rucksack he'd brought along. From inside, he removed a fat bundle of sketches, knotted with hairy string.

Mary said, 'What's this?'

Kenny gave her the bundle. It contained many sketches in charcoal, pencil and watercolour on scraps of paper and envelopes and a few hasty oils on ragged squares of canvas.

The sketches showed Mary laughing over breakfast — the Sally Bowles haircut she'd worn then all askew and kohl smudged under her eyes; Mary with her fringe obscuring her face, frowning as she winds a Felix the Cat clock; Mary barefoot in cotton pyjamas, sipping from a steaming mug.

She'd been a good model — indulgent, patient, entertaining, impervious to cold and cramp.

She flicked through the sketches, chuckling. She had happy, nostalgic tears in her eyes. 'Look at my hair!'

'I liked your hair. You had nice hair.'

She gathered the sketches like playing cards. 'So what's all this in aid of?'

'Nothing. I just thought — they're gathering dust in a drawer. You might as well have them.'

She was toying with the string that had bound the sketches. 'So this would be the point where you come out and tell me what's actually wrong.'

He gave her a big smile. 'Nothing! I'm just sorting things out. I thought — what's the point of me hanging on to these? I thought you might like them.'

'I love them.'

'Good.'

'You should be famous. You're so good.'

He smiled because she was kind. And he knew he couldn't cross Mary off the list today, because he didn't know how to put right what had gone wrong between them a long time ago.

They finished their picnic lunch, then stood to leave because Mary had to get back to work. She kissed Kenny's cheek and squeezed his elbow and said 'Love you', and she ruffled his brush of scruffy white hair.

He said, 'Love you, too.'

And having thus failed to begin putting his affairs in order, Kenny went to catch the bus home.

4

After work, Mary went home to a Victorian terrace on a steep hill in Totterdown — a brightly painted house on a street of brightly painted houses, blue and yellow and green.

She put her bags down in the hallway and looked in on Stever and the kids.

Stever was reading a book of Ray Bradbury short stories; it had a lurid 1970s cover design. Otis and Daisy were watching Cartoon Network.

Mary gave the kids a hug and a kiss and asked how their day had gone, but they didn't say much. That was okay: her real time with them would be later, sitting on the edge of the bath while they soaked, chatting while they dried themselves and got into their pyjamas, reading them stories and playing What Else? with Otis.

She gave Stever a kiss, too. He was in cut-off jeans, rubber flip-flops and a washed-out *Prisoner* T-shirt — Patrick McGoohan's face crazed and faded after years of washing and tumble drying.

Stever had very long hair and a big auburn beard. Back in the early days, Mary had nagged him to shave it off because it tickled when they kissed. He'd sulked a bit, but done as she asked. His face had looked blinking and helpless, so Mary apologized and told him to grow it back. Now the tickle of it was a comfort to her, a sign of house and home and quiet well-being.

She sat with her hands on her knees and her back straight, looking at the screen. Stever glanced at her over his book, then folded the corner of a page and put it down. 'What's wrong?'

He always knew. That was one of the things about him.

She said, 'I met Kenny today. Up by the Cabot Tower.'

Once, Stever and Kenny had been best friends. They used to drive out to the country in Kenny's old VW Combi and fake crop circles together, using planks and lengths of camping rope and tent pegs. They were still friends, although things weren't the same.

Stever said, 'How is he?'

Mary said, 'Come out here a minute?'

Stever frowned and stood, brushed hair from his face, followed Mary to the narrow hall, closing the door on the sound of *Spongebob Squarepants*.

'He gave me these,' Mary said, and showed

Stever the bundle of sketches.

Stever undid the string, shuffled through them. He looked at Mary. 'Why?'

'I don't know.'

'Is he all right?'

'I don't know.'

'Should I go out there and talk to him?'

'He won't talk to you. Not if he won't talk to me. He'll just clam up. He pretends nothing's wrong — especially to us.'

'Well, I ought to give him a buzz. Ask him round. We'll catch a few old vids — *Day of the Dead*, whatever. I'll take him down the New Found Out.'

Mary took Stever's hand in both of hers, lifted it to her face, butterfly-kissed his knuckles. 'Let's leave it a few days.'

'You sure?'

'Yeah. I'll give him a call tomorrow. Make sure he's all right.'

* * *

The next day, Mary called Kenny during her morning break. She phoned him again at lunchtime, and again in the late afternoon, but Kenny didn't answer.

On the bus on the way home, she texted him: 'U OK? X.'

He didn't answer that, either.

* * *

Mary still owned the little black address book she and Kenny had once kept by the phone. The pages were full of addresses added and scored-through over many years. These days, she kept it in a little drawer upstairs.

She dug it out and found the mobile number of a woman called Pat Maxwell. She dialled it, heard a tentative, gruff: 'Hello?'

'Hi, Pat! It's Mary. Kenny Drummond's Mary?'

'Kenny's Mary?'

'You remember?'

'Pretty little Mary with the dark hair?'

Mary was disarmed by that, and wished she wasn't.

Pat said, 'What can I do for you, love?'

'I was wondering if Kenny had been in touch?'

'What — your Kenny?'

'Yes, my Kenny. As was.'

'Not for donkey's years. Why?'

'No reason.'

'You're sure?'

'Well, to be honest we've been a bit worried about him.'

'Why's that?'

'It's nothing, it's silly really.'

‘Silly enough you need to call me? Is it the Kintry business?’

‘No, it’s not that.’

‘You’re sure?’

‘Pretty sure. Pat, I’m sorry. It’s probably nothing. I don’t want to be a pain.’

‘You’re nothing of the sort, love. I’m glad you called. Tell you what I’ll do; if he does get in contact I’ll give you a call. Let you know. How’s that?’

‘That would be great. I mean, it’s probably nothing. But yeah. Thank you.’

‘No problem. How’s the kiddies?’

‘They’re great.’

‘Good for you.’

Mary gave Pat her number, just in case, then hung up.

She’d hoped that hearing Pat’s voice would put her at ease. But it had made things worse.

So had the mention of Thomas Kintry.

5

Thomas Kintry was an 11-year-old West Indian boy who had lived not far away from Kenny and Mary, near Lawrence Hill station. One Saturday morning in 1998, his mother had sent him to the United Supermarkets corner shop because they needed milk for breakfast.

As Thomas walked along Bowers Road, he was approached by a white man driving a small commercial van.

'Mate,' said the man in the van, rolling down the window. 'Mate, excuse me. Have you got a minute?'

Thomas Kintry looked at the pavement and kept walking. He nearly collided with Kenny, who was just stepping out of his front door, leaving early for work.

Usually, Kenny didn't work on Saturdays. He just had a few jobs that needed to be done.

He turned to see the boy hurrying along, staring at the pavement. Then he noticed the van. It was driving slowly.

These two things — the boy moving quickly, the van slow and predatory behind him — made Kenny feel strange.

As the van passed by, the driver turned his head and looked Kenny in the eye. Then the van accelerated, turned right and sped away.

Kenny didn't know what to do.

Had something just happened?

He stood there, feeling foolish, squinting in the low morning sun.

He took a few tentative steps. He walked, then he stopped. He waited, feeling wrong, until he saw the kid enter the corner shop at the end of the road.

Then, relieved, Kenny turned and walked in the other direction, towards the bus-stop.

⋆ ⋆ ⋆

When Thomas Kintry emerged from the corner shop, the van was back. It was waiting for him across the road.

The driver was crossing the quiet street. He said, 'Mate — what's your name?'

'Thomas.'

'Thomas what?'

'Thomas Kintry.'

'Right. I thought it must be you.'

'Why?' said Thomas Kintry.

'I'm sorry, mate. There's been an accident.'

'What kind of accident?'

'You'd better come with me.'

The man was breathing strangely. When Thomas hesitated, the man licked his lips and said, 'I've been sent to take you to your mum. You'd better get in.'

'That's all right, thanks,' said Thomas Kintry.

'Your mum might die,' said the man, trying to lead Thomas Kintry by the elbow. 'You'd better hurry up.'

'That's all right, thanks,' said Thomas Kintry again. He politely tried to shake off the man's rigid hold.

'You'll get me in trouble if I go back without you,' said the man. 'The police sent me to get you. You'll get us both in really bad trouble.'

Thomas Kintry didn't speak. He just pushed on. In one hand, he had a Spar carrier bag containing some semi-skimmed milk and a packet of pickled onion Monster Munch.

The man grabbed Thomas Kintry's skinny shoulder, trying to turn him around and force-march him to the van.

Thomas Kintry tried to run, but the man's grip was too strong. The man began to hustle Thomas Kintry to the van, half-carrying him.

Thomas Kintry wanted to shout out, but he was too embarrassed. He knew you shouldn't shout at grown-ups, no matter what they were doing. He was a very well brought-up child.

* * *

A middle-aged shopkeeper called Pradeesh Jeganathan was watching all this from behind the window of United Supermarkets. He saw the man try to scoop up the skinny little boy and carry him to the van that was parked on the corner. Mr Jeganathan could see blue smoke issuing from the van's exhaust pipe. The man had left the engine idling.

Mr Jeganathan took up the rounders bat he kept under the counter. The handle was wrapped in bright blue duct tape. He ran out, his exit announced by the familiar tinkling of the little bell above the door.

Mr Jeganathan called out, 'You! Mister! You! Van man!'

The man let go of Thomas Kintry.

Thomas Kintry dropped his carrier bag and ran. He ran all the way home.

Mr Jeganathan ran to the van, wielding the rounders bat and roaring at the driver.

Mr Jeganathan got there just in time to whack the man across the shoulders with the rounders bat. He tried to wrestle the man to the floor, but the man — in a panic — bit down on Mr Jeganathan's cheek and then his ear.

Bleeding, Mr Jeganathan was nevertheless still able to smash one of the van's brake-lights before the man pulled away at speed.

Mr Jeganathan stumbled back to the shop, clutching at his bleeding face. First he called the police. Then he had his third heart attack in as many years.

* * *

That night, on the local news, the police made an appeal for witnesses. So Kenny, who had been raised always to do the right thing, went to the police.

They didn't use sketch artists any more. Specially trained officers used facial composite software.

So while Inspector Pat Maxwell looked on, chain smoking, a young police officer asked Kenny to pick out separate features of the driver's face: eyes, mouth, nose. These components would then be assembled into a face.

The police were patient, but Kenny was overwhelmed by choice. Soon, he realized he couldn't remember what the man in the van looked like.

Sensing his anxiety, Pat took him to the pub and said: 'You haven't let anybody down. If you want to know the truth, those composites have got an accuracy rate of about twenty per cent. That's the thing with eyewitness testimony. It's just not very good.'

She told him about a study at Yale University. She said: 'These well-trained, very fit young soldiers were put face-to-face with an interrogator — a really aggressive bastard — for forty-five minutes.'

'Next day, each of them was asked to pick out the interrogator from a line-up. Sixty-eight per cent picked the wrong man. That's after forty-five minutes of face-to-face contact across a table in a well-lit room. You saw this bloke, the man in the van, for two seconds. Three seconds, tops.'

'But what if he's out there now,' said Kenny, 'at the wheel of his van, looking for another little boy? What if that's happening because of me?'

'It's not because of you, or because of anyone else. It's because of him.'

Kenny knew Pat was right, but not in his heart.

The man who tried to abduct Thomas Kintry was never caught.

Kenny had never stopped thinking about it.

6

And now, all these years later, Kenny stood outside Mr Jeganathan's shop, with its green and gold signage. It stood on the corner of a street of bay-fronted Victorian terraces.

It sold newspapers and onions and coconut milk and it smelled of fresh coriander and dusty sunlight. Kenny stood with his back to the picture window, looking across the street — at the spot where the attempted abduction of Thomas Kintry had taken place.

When he opened the shop door, a bell tinkled.

Behind the counter was a very beautiful young woman. She had a pierced nose and was wearing a baggy sweatshirt. She was sitting on a stool behind the counter, looking bored.

When she turned sideways, Kenny saw she was perhaps eight months pregnant.

He said, 'Hi.'

She said 'Hello', and made ready to sell him some tobacco or a Scratch card.

'I'm looking for Pradeesh Jeganathan. Is he around at all?'

The woman stopped. 'Dad passed away, I'm afraid.'

'Oh God,' said Kenny. 'Oh, look. I'm sorry.'

He was about to say something else but was interrupted by the door opening and the bell jingling. An old Rastafarian entered and picked up a shopping basket. Kenny felt the moment slipping away.

The woman gave a sad smile for his obvious bewilderment, but there was delicate, curious flexing between her eyes.

Kenny knew that, to her, anything that happened across the road a decade before belonged to the past. It could never be real to her in the way it was to him.

He thought of Mr Jeganathan, who had beaten him to where he was going.

He said, 'Thanks, anyway', and walked out of the door with the tinkling bell and to the Combi. It was parked in the spot where the white van had parked, idling at the kerb.

* * *

Kenny drove to an industrial park in south-east Bristol. He passed through the gates, got lost, reversed, asked for directions, then parked on a concrete forecourt outside a specialist glass factory.

He walked to the reception, which was in a Portakabin erected outside the plant. He stood at the glass and stainless steel desk and asked if he could speak to Thomas Kintry.

It had been so easy — all it had taken was a visit to Thomas Kintry's Friends Reunited profile, which gave this glass factory as his place of work. Then to the 'About Us' section of the glass factory website to get the address.

He hadn't even been nervous — but he was now, waiting on the sunny forecourt as Thomas Kintry stepped out from beneath a wide aluminium roller door, darkness and noise behind it, and came loping towards him.

Thomas Kintry wore a white T-shirt and blue overalls, heavily stained, the upper part tied round his waist. As he approached, he opened a bottle of mineral water and took a glugging sip.

Then he wiped his mouth with the back of his hand and said, 'Can I help you?'

Kenny was moved by the softness of Thomas Kintry's voice; until that moment, it had been difficult to link this sauntering man with that skinny little boy.

Squinting in the sun, Kenny offered his hand. 'I'm Kenny Drummond.'

Thomas Kintry shook it, polite and

bewildered. 'Have we . . . ?'

'Not really.'

Thomas Kintry smiled in confusion. Kenny wished he'd prepared something to say. He said, 'I'm here to apologize. Sort of.'

'For what?'

'We never actually met. But I was there — the morning it happened.'

'The morning what happened?'

'That man . . . in the van. The one who tried to — '

There was a moment. Thomas Kintry's eyes softened, then brightened — and he understood. He said, 'You're joking me.'

'No.'

'This is about that time on Bowers Road? When I was little?'

'Yes.'

'Were you there?'

'Sort of . . . '

But Thomas Kintry was working it out, replaying it behind his eyes. 'So you're the man I bumped into, right? On the doorstep? Ken, was it? Dennis?'

'Kenny.'

Thomas Kintry clapped once and pointed. 'Kenny!' Then he said, 'And you're here to what . . . ?'

'Say sorry.'

'For what?'

'I couldn't remember what the man looked like.'

'Shit,' said Thomas Kintry — exhilarated by this unexpected connection between them. 'You can't have seen him for more than, like, two seconds or something. All he did was drive past.'

'But I'm a portrait painter. I'm good at faces.'

They stood there in the ringing sunlight.

Thomas Kintry grew calm. 'I couldn't remember what he looked like, either. They had this specialist. But I couldn't remember anything, except he was wearing this really cheesy pair of trainers — like Asda trainers, yeah?'

Kenny laughed at that; they both did.

Then Thomas Kintry said, 'You've got nothing to feel sorry for.'

'I let you down. You were just a little boy. I could have done better.'

'But even I don't think about all that, not any more. It was such a long time ago.'

Thomas Kintry wore a small, gold crucifix around his neck and now his hand went to it. He tugged it left and right on the chain. His expression changed. 'Come here a minute.'

Kenny followed him, stepping out of the sunlight and away from the glass factory. Thomas Kintry led him to a low brick wall with grass growing through cracks. It wasn't far from a specialist doll's house manufacturer that had recently closed down.

Thomas Kintry sat on the low wall. He sat on his hands, like a child. 'The sun was hurting my eyes.'

Kenny knew it was really to get out of the way of inquiring workmates. Thomas Kintry looked at Kenny and said, 'Are you okay?'

The gentle concern in his voice made Kenny helpless. He sat there for quite a while, blinking. He didn't know what to say.

'My mum,' Thomas Kintry told him, 'when she gets really down, she churns over the past. All the things she thinks she did wrong, all the people she let down. There was this one Christmas when the turkey came out too dry; she still goes on about that bloody turkey, what a miserable Christmas day it was. And this is, like — 1993 or something. But she still goes on about it. My nan was the same.'

Kenny nodded.

In a lower, more emphatic voice Thomas Kintry said: 'I don't blame anyone that he was never caught. Not the police, definitely not you. All you were was an eyewitness. It never even occurred to me that you'd done less than you could. The only one to blame was that bloke, whoever he was. And even he's not someone I think about very much.'

In the lull that followed, Thomas Kintry polished the crucifix softly between thumb and forefinger and was far away. Then he laughed and let go of the crucifix. 'And I bet Mr Jeganathan from the corner shop made him think twice about trying it again.'

Kenny smiled, thinking about it. 'So. You doing all right for yourself?'

'I'm doing all right, yeah. Can't complain.'

'What is it you do?'

'Architectural glass. Commercial, domestic, whatever. You should come, have a look round. The stuff we do, it's unbelievable.'

'How'd you get into that?'

'I don't know, really. My nan had this piece of Bristol blue. You ever seen Bristol blue glass?'

Kenny nodded. It was a deep bright blue, the blue of old medicine bottles.

'My granddad told me, it's because the glass had cobalt oxide and lead oxide in it. You hold it up to the light, it's lovely. So it was then, I suppose. I liked doing science, I liked doing art. It just seemed to go together.'

Kenny nodded.

'You want to come in, have a look round? I'll give you the guided tour.'

'Thanks. But I'd better let you get back to it.'

'You'd be welcome.'

'That's all right. I'll let you get back to it. But it was really nice to meet you.'

'You, too,' said Thomas Kintry. 'Are you sure you're okay?'

'I'm sure. I'm fine.'

Thomas Kintry toyed with the crucifix for a moment, as if uncertain. Then he said, 'It matters to me that you came here today. Thank you.'

He offered his hand and Kenny shook it — warmly this time, the way good friends shake hands, or father and son. Kenny wanted to say thank you in return, but couldn't. Instead, he just nodded.

Then Thomas Kintry turned and walked away, overalls tied about his waist, water bottle in his hand, sunlight glinting from the gold chain round his neck.

* * *

At home, Kenny sat for a long time with the list in his hand, the folds of it sweat-stained and translucent.

It read:

Mary
~~Mr Jeganathan~~
~~Thomas Kintry~~
Callie Barton

Kenny thought about Callie Barton. Some time passed. Then he went to the wide, low portfolio drawer, the same drawer from which he'd taken the portraits of Mary. Alone in the bottom was a dusty buff envelope. From inside it, he withdrew an old class photograph.

It showed three rows of children wearing the haircuts and clothes of the late 1970s. Kenny was there, centre middle row, wearing a zip-up cardigan. He was grinning and his dandelion hair stuck up at the crown.

Bottom right was a skinny girl. She wore a navy-blue jersey, flared jeans, Dunlop Greenflash trainers, a pageboy haircut. She was smiling for the camera. That was her.

7

Kenny had been a small, cheerful child who wore strange clothes — they'd been rooted out in CND jumble sales and from the tables in the Spastics' shop and were always just wrong enough: flowery shirts with extravagant double cuffs, noisy checked bell-bottoms, plastic sandals.

The kids at school ridiculed his strange appearance and his weird smell and his jaunty demeanour. They called him Happy Drummond. He didn't know it was an insult.

The kids at school also said Kenny's dad was a loony — that he went down the greengrocer's naked but for an army-surplus greatcoat and orange flip-flops.

His dad was Aled Drummond. Kenny's mum was Carol. She died when Kenny was two, which is when Aled began his struggle with lunacy, alternating bouts of depression with long spells of exhilarated, perfect elation.

His body was sapling-narrow — skinny hips, long legs with knotty knees and big splayed feet. He was carrot-topped and beak-nosed and, in his madness, grey-bearded and regal — like a refugee in his military greatcoat and hobnailed boots.

As far as Kenny could remember, it had always been the two of them. Sometimes their privacy was compromised by a social worker. She was quiet and earnest, a good woman who meant well and wanted to help.

She began to visit because sometime in the mid-1970s, it became clear that Aled was suffering from what was still called manic depression. He lost his job in the Housing Department, went on Sickness Benefit, then became a full-time potter, setting up a wheel in the little garden shed. After the winter of 1977 he moved the wheel into the back room, by the kitchen, where it was warmer.

At the crest of his mania, Aled would talk — riff, really; it was like listening to the most delirious kind of jazz.

'Of all the boys in all the world,' he'd say, in his big Welsh voice, much too big for his spindly body, 'of all the children who ever were, God and fate — all of history! the entire world! — brought you to me, like Moses in his little basket.'

There were hours and days and weeks of this. It seemed to Kenny that Aled's madness was accompanied always by bright, clean sunlight.

Their little terraced house in Fishponds was a chaos of half-random paraphernalia — potter's wheels and painty sheets, splattered knives, cracked mugs and hand-made plates. It was never clean.

Aled bought things they couldn't afford. He had a passion for Matchbox cars, books about King Arthur and Welsh mythology. They went on train trips to Toy Collector fairs in Birmingham, London, Stratford-upon-Avon. Aled took him to places on the bus — the zoo, the museum, galleries, art collectives, performance workshops, the Glastonbury Free Festival at Worthy Farm.

Or they'd just stand side-by-side in the back room, happily syncopated, Kenny slapping gouache on to reused canvas until the good light was gone and the night drew near; Aled on his stool, forming pots from clay like God forming Adam.

Aled read aloud to him — stories of Arthur and Merlin and Camelot; the *Red Book of Hergest*; the *Book of Taliesin*. He told him of Culhwch, a hero cursed to marry none but the radiant Olwen, daughter of a terrible giant. He taught Kenny the qualities required by a hero.

When it was dark, Kenny watched TV and dozed. Sometimes Aled hunched next to him, scribbling epic poetry. When Kenny woke in the morning they would both still be there: Kenny gummy-mouthed and blanketed in a trench coat that smelled of pipe tobacco and sweat; Aled transcribing lunatic dictation in small, busy letters on reams of typing paper which later he'd gather in armfuls and shuffle like cards into what seemed like some semblance of order. He hunted out connection and coincidence and — finding them — saw the hand of Providence.

⋆ ⋆ ⋆

When Kenny was eight years old, his teacher sat him and Callie Barton together on a field trip to Glastonbury. The other kids laughed at Callie for being Happy Drummond's boyfriend and having to hold his hand when they crossed the road.

But from that day, Callie Barton was Kenny's best friend.

She didn't speak to him very often and never played with him at lunchtime; mostly, she played elastics with Judith and Isabel and Alison.

But she'd look at him sometimes, across the desks. And when Kenny looked back she'd smile, sweetly and secretly.

⋆ ⋆ ⋆

In the school year that began September 1979, Kenny was nearly ten.

He entered Room 5 to discover their new teacher, Miss Pippenger, had her own way of arranging a classroom.

Near the back, under the big windows, she had positioned three desks, making a kind of square. Around this square would sit six of the cleverest kids. It was because they could be relied on to work quietly; the noisy kids would be kept at front.

Miss Pippenger sat Kenny Drummond and Callie Barton next to each other — so close, Kenny could smell the Vosene in her hair.

They didn't really speak, but sometimes from the corner of his eye Kenny spied her skinny white wrist with its delicate blue veins, and her skinny right hand with its pointy little knuckles, clasped round an HB pencil, chewed at the top. She'd be writing her name at the top of the page, or the date. Writing words, numbers. Sometimes there would be flowers in the margins; sea-horses, ponies, arcs of glitter, rainbows.

* * *

At the end of the fourth week, Callie Barton got stuck on a piece of long division: $435 \div 25$.

Kenny became aware of her anxious stillness, the pressure of the unmoving Staedtler pencil making a dint in the page of her exercise book.

Kenny took a deep breath, gathering the courage he knew was inside him, and leaned in close. They were almost ear to ear. Without speaking, he pushed his exercise book near enough for her to copy. He could hear her breathing as she concentrated.

She whispered: 'Thank you.'

Then she hooked her ankle round his.

Kenny peeped sideways. She was concentrating on her exercise book as if nothing was different.

After lunch, she sat down and hooked her ankle round his again.

She didn't say a word or look at him. Kenny had never been so happy.

⋆ ⋆ ⋆

On Valentine's day, Callie Barton received four cards. She giggled and huddled with her friends.

Kenny had made her a card. He'd painted sunflowers and roses in a green vase and composed a six-line poem. But he never sent the card; it was still under his bed.

When Izzy made a joke about one of

Callie's cards being from stinky old Happy Drummond, Callie said: 'Just shut up and leave him alone.'

They teased her for it, for being nice about Happy Drummond, for being in love with him, for wanting to marry him — and for weeks their derision compelled her to pass over Kenny as if he wasn't there.

But even that didn't stop her secretly crossing ankles with him under the desk, glancing at him sometimes through the corner of her eye, sharing her spelling workbook.

Miss Pippenger would also be their teacher in the final year of junior school. Kenny had the summer holidays of 1980 to reflect on the time he had left at Callie Barton's side.

Time was a dirty river, it carried things away. Next year, he and Callie Barton would no longer be big kids in a little school; they'd be little kids in a big school; wearing navy-blue blazers with badges on the breast pocket.

Kenny was attuned to the nature of endings. Childhood was a permanent ache of nostalgia, of perpetual loss and transformation. He'd learned to sip at moments like they were Ribena, to savour them.

On the first morning of the new term, he walked to school with his scuffed satchel on his back. He walked slowly — knowing this was the last morning of its kind there would ever be.

He passed through the school gates and saw the same faces, all of them subtly altered — different haircuts, different clothes. Some kids had grown up or out; their feet had swollen and elongated; their hands had widened, their necks were long and gangling. Some had longer hair, some had cut it short; some wore new trainers, Puma and Adidas, or they wore new button badges on their Harringtons: The Jam, Madness, the Selecter.

Callie Barton wasn't in the playground.

Callie wasn't there when the bell went, and Callie wasn't there when Kenny filed inside the waxy, feet-smelling school building.

And Callie wasn't sitting at their shared desk; Gary Bishop had been moved up there instead. He'd got some new glasses over the holidays, and short hair that wasn't quite a crew cut.

Seeing Gary Bishop in Callie Barton's chair made Kenny want to vomit, but he said nothing, set down his satchel, said hello and stared at Miss Pippenger.

He didn't know Miss Pippenger was calling the register until she'd spoken his name for a third time — *Kenneth Drummond?* — and the class, those familiar faces changing shape all around him, began to laugh.

* * *

Kenny's heart was laid waste. He found consolation only in the stories by which Aled had educated him — stories that took place in enchanted castles east of the sun and west of the moon; tales of Grail Knights, farm-boy heroes who were brave and pure, lost princesses who slept an enchanted sleep for a hundred years, until a chaste kiss awoke them.

They were stories of imprisonment and transformation — of men into beasts and beasts into men. All that remained constant was youth and beauty and love.

Because of these stories — and because of Aled's noble, shattered heart — Kenny knew about love. Love turned farm boys into kings; love conquered ogres and dragons.

Stored in his heart like a seed, it could only send out roots and grow old and strong. But to speak it would break the spell, crack the glass, see it wither and die.

Kenny's love for Callie Barton was to him the most solemn and sacred of all things. And so he never spoke of it. But he thought of her often — this little girl who showed him compassion, then silently withdrew from his world.

* * *

Kenny looked at the class photograph for a long time. Then he slipped it back into the envelope and returned it to the empty portfolio drawer.

He went to his laptop and, with a fluttering stomach and a dryness in his mouth, searched on Friends Reunited and Facebook and everywhere else he could think of, looking for a mention of Callie Barton.

He searched and searched. But she wasn't there.

8

It almost sounded like Pat Maxwell had been expecting Kenny to call; she knew it was him at once. 'Well, hello there, Rembrandt.'

Hearing her fag-raddled voice, Kenny was struck by vivid nostalgia. He asked if he could pop round and see her.

She told him she'd moved years ago, not long after retiring.

Time. It just went.

* * *

Now Kenny was standing outside a mobile home — a big double-width caravan on Worlebury Hill, overlooking Weston-super-Mare.

It was an old holiday let — a little dilapidated; the colour of clotted cream, with coffee-coloured trim — that stood permanently moored on a grassy flat, hedged in by rowan and crab apple. It had a good view of Weston — the long, empty crescent of muddy beach.

He stood on the step, unsure of mobile home etiquette, until Pat tugged the door open.

Kenny was disconcerted to see she'd become an old woman in gardening clothes and a cardigan that drooped at her hips like a dewlap. Her stern haircut was blunt across the brow, streaked with white. But still, that copper's scowl.

She said, 'Come in. I'll do us a brew', and he followed her. Inside, it was orange and caramel. There was a portable TV, a litter tray, not much else. It smelled of gas and cats.

Pat stood in the kitchenette and made them a cup of milky tea, pale as a winter dawn. Cats curled tight to her ankles and calves, and then to Kenny's.

He said, 'So how've you been?'

'Oh, y'know. Life of Riley.'

He saw in her face that she was happy here but embarrassed to admit it. People sometimes didn't like to admit to being happy because what made them happy wasn't grandeur and passion; it wasn't love and sex and money, but simple things that others might not understand — a small garden, a ready supply of cigarettes, a cup of good tea, model trains in the attic, afternoon trips to empty cinemas.

Kenny said, 'So, what've you been up to?'

'What do you think? I sit round on my arse all day. Bit of weeding, read the papers. Crafty fag. If that's all right.'

He knew not to blink as she assessed his response. He and Pat had the same skills, the same talent for faces. Right now she was reading him, weighing his intentions.

She said: 'So how's the painting?'

'It's a living.'

'It's a gift from God. You look after it. I heard your Mary got married again.'

'She's happy.'

'For the best, then.'

'For the best.'

Sipping tea, he followed her outside. They stood on the long grass, insulated by the hedges from the hillside road.

Pat said: 'So what do you want?'

'To find someone.'

'Don't we all.'

He let that hang in the air until she said: 'Find who?'

'A girl. From my school. My junior school.'

'Because . . . ?'

'She was nice to me. When I was a kid. She was the only one that was. I want to tell her — well, that I never forgot.'

'And that's it?'

'Pretty much.'

'Why?'

'Because if you do something kind, you should know that it mattered.'

'Then look on the whatsit, internet. Google

her. That's what they all do.'

'I tried that.'

'Well, it's easy enough to find someone that's not trying to hide. You got details?'

'I know the street she lived on. Her surname. Year of birth. Stuff like that.'

'Then you could do it yourself. Give me a pen. I'll write down what to do.'

'I don't have time.'

'Then hire someone. I can give you a name. Get you a rate.'

'I'd really like you to do it.'

'Why?'

'Because it's private.'

He held her gaze.

'She'll be married,' said Pat. 'Or divorced. She'll have kids. She'll be dyeing her hair because she's going grey. She'll have varicose veins and her tits will be round her ankles. Whoever she is, she's not that little girl any more. She's what that little girl turned into.' Her face relaxed and she said, 'When I was ten, I studied ballet.'

She gestured at her body — potato shaped, thick-ankled. Kenny grinned politely.

She told him: 'I can't find that girl for you. She's gone.'

'I know that.'

'Then what's the point? You're young. Things like this, dreams of dead days, it's an old man's game. Leave it be.'

'I'm dying.'

In the silence that followed, she searched his face. At length, she sighed. 'Cancer, is it?'

'In the brain.'

'How long they give you?'

'A few weeks.'

She was the first person he'd told. It had sounded strange, coming out of his mouth — but it hadn't sounded momentous, either, or even that important.

'Well, it's a shame. You're a very nice man.'

'Thank you.'

'And it'll be my pleasure to help you.'

He fumbled and blushed. 'How much do you think . . . ?'

'Just give me a painting. One of your favourites — a nice landscape or something. A sunset. Something to hang on my wall. Who knows, it might be worth something — when you're gone.'

They laughed.

She took his phone number, his street address, his email address. Then she wrote down all the details he had to give her.

As Kenny walked back to the car, he could feel her in the doorway, watching him, cats coiling round her ankles.

He felt good, as if he had finally embarked on a long journey.

9

The next day, Pat drove to Bristol and met Paul Sugar in a café off the Gloucester Road.

She'd known Paul since he was fresh out of Hendon Police College. In those days, he'd looked like Nazi propaganda — broad shouldered, blue-eyed, blond haired.

As a police officer, Paul never came across a backhander that wasn't worth pocketing or a blow job that wasn't worth having. He'd lasted five years and was fortunate, in the end, to avoid prison.

Now he was forty-four, a mastiff of a man. The same bright blue eyes lost in a grossly wattled face; his little remaining blond hair cropped and baby-soft. His shoulders were not just broad but huge. He wore a three-button suit and an open-necked shirt; his heavy belly strained against it.

As he moved his hands with considered delicacy, opening sachets of sugar, pouring them into his coffee, Pat could hear the gentle wheeze of his breathing.

Paul was a private detective, marital and corporate work mostly.

Pat said, 'It's a day's work, tops.'

Paul licked crumbs from his fingers: 'You've got name, DOB, last known address?'

She gave him the piece of paper.

Paul scanned it. 'To you, that'll be seven hundred.'

'I didn't ask for a vial of George Clooney's semen. This is kids' stuff.'

'Then do it yourself.'

'I'm too tired. My knees hurt. There's gardening to do and *Countdown* to watch. All you have to do is find this woman, tell me where she lives, who she married. Get a trainee to do it.'

'The trainee left. Call it five hundred, cash.'

'Two hundred.'

'Two-fifty.'

'Fine. Two-fifty.'

'Payment up front.'

'Up my arse. Two hundred and fifty quid when you deliver.'

* * *

She left Paul to his latte and drove up Stapleton Road. She parked, then walked to Hartledge & Kassel.

These days, an ugly metal grille was fixed to the windows and on display were beige Dell computers and inline skates and stereos and wristwatches — but it was the same old pawn broker and the bell still tinkled when Pat went inside.

She didn't recognize the balding young man behind the glass counter, so she said, 'Hello. Are you a Hartledge or a Kassel?'

He looked up from his newspaper, blinking. 'A Kassel, for my sins. Dave.'

Having decided Pat was neither a gangster nor from the Inland Revenue, Dave Kassel extended a hand. Pat shook it, saying: 'I knew your Dad. Harry.'

'Harry was my granddad.'

'Was he really?'

She tutted. Then she began to pat down her pockets. 'I used to be a copper. I'd come in here when I was a nipper in uniform. Your dad — your granddad — he always had the kettle on. Lovely old chap.'

'He helped a bit, did he? With your inquiries and that?'

'He shared a bit of tittle-tattle now and again. Small-talk, over a cuppa.'

They shared a complicit look.

'Different days,' said Pat. 'Dead days, long gone.'

From her pocket she removed a thin gold ring. She'd been twenty-one when her Aunt Ettie left it to her. But in the end, it was only a thing — and really, who had use for things?

She held it up so the cider-coloured sun

glinted from it. 'How much for this, then?'

Dave Kassel examined it with quick fingers and a skilled eye.

Pat said: 'Don't piss me around now. I need two hundred and fifty quid. The ring's Victorian. If it ends up going to auction, God forbid, you'll get twice that.'

Dave Kassel hesitated. Then he laid aside the loupe that had been halfway to his eye; a nice bit of theatre.

He gave Pat a stiff, almost clerical bow. 'Two fifty it is.' He went rummaging for the receipt book.

'Actually,' Pat said, 'make it two seventy-five.'

She might as well treat herself to fish and chips on the way home, perhaps a nice bottle of something.

She'd sit on the step, the cats around her. She'd watch the sun go down and she'd raise a glass to long lost, dizzy-in-love, never forgotten Auntie Ettie, wherever she might be.

10

Stever believed that everyone should be allowed one perfect summer. His had been the summer of 1989, the year he and Kenny began faking crop circles.

The designs were simple at first. Giggling and shushing each other in the darkness, they flattened the grain clockwise using a plank and a nylon tow-rope that had been secured to the ground with a tent peg.

They'd drink cider, smoke a few spliffs and almost piss themselves laughing. They'd watch the sunrise, then catch an hour's sleep in the back of Kenny's Combi.

It was also the summer that Kenny met Mary — which meant it was the summer Stever met Mary, too. He was smitten more or less at first sight, spellbound by her Louise Brooks haircut, her pale skin, her green eyes, her Marlboro Reds and Chuck Taylors.

Soon, she was conspiring with them to compose ever more elaborate crop circle designs — petal formations, interlocking Koch fractals, the Eye of Horus.

That summer — and for more than one summer after that — it seemed to Stever that every song ever written had been written about her.

That had been the year they all turned twenty. Which is what Stever was thinking about when he fired up Google Mail and wrote:

To: Kdrummond467@gmail.com From: STEVER.BEEZER@gmail.com
Subject: WHERE'S EE TO THEN?

Kenny My Babber

Long time no see!

Mary's been trying to get in contact. Nothing urgent though she's a bit vexed. She likes to worry, it gives her something to do.

Anyway I'm sure you're fine and all that. I've tried to call a couple of times. But you're not returning my calls either, which frankly is just rude.

Get your priorities right and give us a call then!

Stever. (Remember?)

His finger hovered over the keyboard for a moment. He pressed 'Send' before he could over-think it. Then he ambled off to get a beer, trying not to worry.

But to Stever, the future was a dark wood in which lurked unspeakable things. He couldn't help it.

11

Three days later, Pat met Paul Sugar in the same café. He gave her the information. In return, she slipped him an envelope containing two hundred and fifty pounds in cash.

Paul was immense, hangdog, commiserating. 'What can I say? I'm sorry. It's just the way of the world.'

When he'd gone, Pat stuffed the information — summarized on a laser-printed sheet of A4 — into her handbag.

She popped into the King's Head for old times' sake, had a quick Jameson's.

Nobody recognized her.

* * *

With the two hundred and fifty pounds deposited in his pocket, Paul Sugar parked behind P. Sugar Private Investigations Ltd, which currently occupied three rooms above a dry cleaner's on Fishponds Road.

Before going in, he slipped a twenty from the envelope and popped to the chemist. He bought a box of Imodium, a bottle of Pepto

Bismol and a tube of 1 per cent hydrocortisone cream.

He popped two Imodium in the street, swallowing them with a scowl before they could dissolve on his tongue and leave him tasting them until Christmas. Then he trudged up to the office.

He'd left Steph — his PA and sole remaining member of staff — to man the phones, but hadn't been expecting any calls. It had been a quiet week. It had been a quiet month. It had been a quiet year.

A mute glance from Steph, reading *Heat* behind her desk, confirmed that no miracles had taken place during his brief absence.

Paul didn't know what phenomena lay beneath this deathly silence. But whatever it was, it was killing him.

The previous autumn, in order to stay in business, he'd set aside all private foreboding and enacted the Doomsday Plan: he'd blackmailed a former client, the wealthiest client who ever employed him. He offered to keep the photographs of her daughter off the internet for a few more years.

The client had wept. Paul sat there, embarrassed, wanting to hold her hand or something. Eventually she got hold of herself and spat in his face. After that, she paid him enough to cover rent and wages for half a year, if he economized.

None of this came without personal cost: Paul developed migraines and his childhood eczema came back — there were scaly, vermilion patches inside his wrists, elbows and ankles; weeping blotches on his chest; a flaking, oozing neighbourhood inside his pubic hair.

The last three times Paul got laid, he'd been obliged to poke the old Hamilton through the gap in his underwear. He knew there weren't many things in the world less sexy than a cheerfully pink erection jabbing through the vent in a fat man's Y-fronts. But what could he do?

The blackmail had temporarily kept P. Sugar Private Investigations Ltd afloat, but Paul was still running on fumes. Week by week, he watched the supply of sullied money run lower and lower, and became more and more unwell.

Then the engine of his business sputtered and died and he was cut adrift, not knowing how to do anything else.

He was too scared to exercise the Doomsday Plan again; he thought the self-hatred might kill him. So instead he paid a visit to a loan shark called Edward Burrell.

* * *

To fill his days, Edward Burrell still cut hair — half price for pensioners, Monday to Thursday; half price for the under-tens, who got a lollipop for sitting still. Wash, cut and blow dry from £7.50. Lesbians went there to get flat-tops.

But he'd been a Shylock since before the Watergate scandal. Paul had known him for years, had even done some work for him. Which is why Burrell agreed to lend him twenty thousand pounds, every penny of which faded away like desire after orgasm.

Paul was left up to his ears in the worst kind of debt. He considered running away. But he didn't, because he couldn't afford to.

So he drove out to Edward Burrell's house and explained himself — money was short, times were hard. He evoked their long history of co-operation and friendship.

Two of Burrell's boys threw Paul in the back of a Commer van and drove him to a quiet place, where they kicked the shit out of him without fear of interruption.

* * *

Paul sold his car to make the next payment, replacing it with a 17-year-old Honda Accord for which he paid seventy-five pounds. Paul was five sizes too big for it. He squeezed behind the wheel like an elephant in a cartoon.

He lay awake at night, scratching himself as the debt to Edward Burrell silently divided and spread like frost on a windowpane.

As he applied hydrocortisone to the weeping skin between his nipples, he brooded on the kind of action he knew he'd have to take in order to free himself of these vexations.

He wondered how long you could feel shame for the kind of deed committed when there was absolutely no choice. There was a limit, surely?

He totted up the worst things he'd ever done and went to some mental effort, tabulating how long he'd felt truly bad about the very worst of them. After some deliberation, he arrived at a maximum of five years.

That seemed credible. It represented a lot of Imodium Plus and a lot of hydrocortisone cream and a lot of looking in the mirror and despising what you saw. But it was way better than the alternative.

Whatever was required, Paul knew he could do it.

Scratching his chest, he could look himself in the eye and feel a strange kind of dignity — and know his moment was coming, screaming towards him like a locomotive down a long tunnel. All he had to do was grab it, jump on board, not be dashed on the tracks as it passed.

12

It was Wednesday morning, not quite 9 a.m., and it was raining. Weston's sea-front arcades and souvenir shops were still shut. A westerly wind carried the faint scent of chips, vinegar, a hundred years of candy floss.

A couple of kids were scootering along the promenade. Ancient couples sat in bus shelters.

Kenny stepped on to the Grand Pier. It had been around since Edward VII, and the boards underfoot seemed rattletrap and loose; he could imagine the entire structure cracking down the centre like a traumatized femur.

He walked past men who leaned on the railings looking out to where the sea should be. They squinted in the rain, the wind blowing in their hair. Kenny wondered what was going through their minds.

At the end of the pier, the amusement arcade was clamorous and deserted. Inside was a ghost train, a crazy house, one-armed bandits; all unchanged for decades.

It was cold, and he wished he'd bought a baseball cap to keep the rain off. His white hair was ottered to his scalp. He huddled into his windcheater and looked back at the town.

Then he turned to face the other way, and saw the faint blue haze off the Welsh coast. Kenny had never been to Wales. From here, it looked like a foreign country: Annwn, the land of departed souls. And Weston-super-Mare, this Edwardian pier, was a way station, a departure point for the dead.

Pat had said to meet here at 9 a.m.

Kenny was early, because he couldn't sleep. So he huddled, waiting in the rain, until Pat appeared in jeans, white unbranded trainers, a blue anorak. He experienced a wash of tenderness for her, bordering on love — she looked so slow and crabby and helpless in the rain, just another old person in this town of old people.

He said, 'Morning.'

She gave him a look. He saw pity in it, and grew scared.

They went to a coffee concession that was just opening then strolled down the pier.

Now and again the sun peeked out and reflected like a diamond on a passing car. Already, some cars had parked at the south end of the beach. Inside them were people with flasks and picnic breakfasts. They would sit inside those cars all day, if need be — and promenade in the blustering wind, wincing in the scouring sand.

Pat and Kenny found a bench. They sat close, almost touching.

He didn't speak, just sat waiting, not wanting to hear it. At length, Pat said, 'Okay. Callie Barton's parents were Ted and Alice. She was an only child, late and unexpected. By all accounts, they treated her like a princess.

'Ted was some kind of manager at one of those petrochemical companies, up in Avonmouth. He took his family to London in 1980 because he'd been promoted.'

'So that's where she went. London.'

'London, then Singapore. Came back to England in 'eighty-nine. Callie did Tax Accountancy at Poole College. Ninety-four, she took a job with a little accountancy firm in Bath. Ninety-seven, she met the man she married.'

Kenny's stomach lurched at those words. He took a moment to steady himself.

Pat said: 'You okay?'

'I'm fine. Coffee on an empty stomach.'

He watched a seagull strut, a few feet away, mangy and arrogant. Its head was velvet and snowy; in the grey light it seemed to fluoresce with a blue-white chemical glow.

The gull was joined by another. They clacked over a scrap of something gristly.

Kenny watched the surprising span of their wings, heard their deranged cawing.

'So where is she? How many kids? Is she happy?'

Pat sipped coffee. 'No kids.'

'No? Did they have problems?'

'Fertility problems?'

'Whatever.'

'Not that I'm aware of. Medical records aren't accessible. But I do know she was admitted to hospital in 2004.'

'Was she ill?'

Pat sucked on her dentures, then reached into her anorak for her cigarettes.

'Broken wrist, fractured orbit of her left eye. Cracked ribs. Scratch on her lung.'

'How do you know this — if medical records are off limits?'

'These aren't medical records, love.' She let him think about it, then gave up. 'They're police records.'

He'd crushed the waxed paper cup and was moving it between his hands like a ball. 'What happened?'

'What happens to most women. She married the wrong man.'

By now, the two gulls had been joined by a third: a flock of seagulls. It made him think of a song, something about wishing for a photograph. Then he laughed a bitter laugh.

'Jesus Christ, Pat. Did they lock him up?'
'She never pressed charges.'
'Why not?'
'They just never do.'
'So where's she now? Is she happy?'
Pat had smoked her cigarette to the halfway point. She crushed it between thumb and index finger, placing the butt in her anorak pocket. 'June 2004. Callie Barton's husband was interviewed about her disappearance.'
The pier was moving in muscular waves beneath Kenny's feet. He supposed it was the tidal current sucking at the steel piles that kept the pier anchored in the estuarine clay.
'What do you mean 'disappearance'?'
'Just that. One day, she's there. Next day, she's not. She just vanishes. The husband was interviewed four times, but no charges were ever brought. Insufficient evidence. It was all in the papers and whatnot . . . '
'What's his name? The husband. Who is he?'
'I'm not telling you his name. What good would it do?'
'If I don't have a name, I can't give him a face.'
'He doesn't deserve a face.'
The tide was tugging harder at the pier now: the entire structure jolted to the left. For a moment, Kenny feared it would collapse.

Then he remembered the tide was out. There was no tide yanking at it. He closed his eyes and his hand, blind and urgent, sought Pat's.

He bent double, hissing through his teeth, saying something that sounded like *gak*.

Pat took his hand. 'What can I do?'

'Just stay.'

A convulsion threw him on to the deck. Pat squatted at his side, holding his hand, talking to him, reassuring him as he writhed and juddered.

She stayed until it had passed and he lay curled on the ground.

Watching them were all those lonely men, men with the wind in the remains of their hair.

Pat looked at them and said with the voice of unfaded authority: 'Piss off out of it. All of you. On your way, now.'

Ashamed, they looked elsewhere.

* * *

Kenny told her he didn't need a doctor. What was the point? He wasn't getting better.

Pat argued for a while, then gave up. She gave Kenny her anorak, because it was longer than his windcheater and would hide most of the urine stain on his trousers.

She drove him to the Combi. At the wheel, she said: 'You'll leave this thing alone. Worrying about this is no way to spend your last days.'

He said, 'Of course.'

He was lying, but felt no guilt. He didn't have time for guilt.

13

Kenny slept eighteen hours and rose the next afternoon feeling cleansed and invigorated, like mountain air after a violent storm.

Stripped to the waist and barefoot in pyjama trousers, he made coffee and sat down at his laptop.

He knew he was looking for local news stories which dated from around June 2004 to around June 2005. They would involve a missing local woman whose first name was Callie or Caroline.

Even so, he didn't find it straight away. First, he had to endure the smiling snapshots of other dead and missing women. But he was persistent; in the end, he found it.

'PHONE HOME'

HUSBAND'S EMOTIONAL PLEA TO MISSING WIFE

The husband of missing Bath woman Caroline Reese, 34, today issued an emotional plea for her to get in touch with her family so that he can 'start picking up the pieces of my life'.

Husband Jonathan Reese's plea comes

six weeks after Callie apparently failed to return home after a night out with friends.

Reese, a landscape gardener, has been questioned by Avon and Somerset police for several days and was subsequently released without charge.

A police spokeswoman said that the police are treating the disappearance as a missing person case at this stage but refused to rule out foul play.

In his statement, issued through a solicitor, Reese said that he just wanted to know that his wife was safe.

'I don't need to know where Caroline is. I just want to know she's safe and happy. It is my profound wish for Caroline to come home. But if she feels she must stay away, I wish she would just let me know she is safe, so I can start picking up the pieces of my life.'

Kenny read the article three times before allowing his eyes to settle on the picture which ran with it.

The photograph, a snapshot really, was zoomed and cropped to make a portrait. It showed a dark-haired and pretty woman, smiling into the sun. Her teeth were even and her squinting eyes were pleasantly crinkled. She wore a baseball cap and had a ponytail.

Underneath was the caption: 'Missing: Caroline Reese'.

Kenny had a passing moment of strange fulfilment. Behind the adult face, this was the girl from the class photograph.

Next, Kenny scrutinized the face of the husband, whose name he now knew to be Jonathan Reese. Lean, dark curly hair cropped short. The photographer had captured him outside a police station, looking gaunt and anxious and hunted.

Kenny went to the bathroom and threw up.

He rinsed with mouthwash, then returned to the computer to Google: LANDSCAPE DESIGN + BATH + REESE.

This led him to the rather dated-looking website of a company called Bath Garden Landscapes.

The home page displayed a stylized, semi-architectural sketch of an idyllic English garden. Down the left of the screen ran a number of hyperlinks.

The first was 'About Us'. Kenny clicked through and read:

Bath Garden Landscapes is Bath's leading landscape gardeners, catering for commercial and private customers. We cover all aspects of landscaping and tree surgery, including paving, fencing, water features, timber decking, driveways . . .

He stopped reading to look over the remaining hyperlinks. 'Garden Design and Process' . . . 'Planting Plans' . . . 'Concept Design'.

Finally, right at the bottom, he found 'Contact Us'.

The page read: Jonathan Reese, 25 Coney Lane, Bath BA2 1JP. It listed a company email address, landline and mobile telephone number. It gave Kenny all the information he needed, but none of the knowledge.

He wondered what he was doing, sitting there in his pyjamas with the sour taste of vomit and mouthwash burning his throat.

He wiggled his head, hoping to see the reflection of his face on the glossy computer monitor. But all he saw was movement — the deep grey shadows of his head and shoulders silhouetted on the screen. His face was a shadow over hers, like a cloud passing over a sunlit hill.

He saw that Pat was right — that little girl was gone, and had been gone for many years. All that remained was a radiant particle of memory; a sprite captured in the round of his skull. She was nothing but a web of connections between his synapses, a web soon to dissolve because the vessel containing it would be empty, just a hollow skull.

Time was running out.

He knew it was his duty to rescue Callie Barton. She was his Guinevere, taken into darkness by the King of the Summer Country. It was his charge to reach into the darkness, find her hand and bring her back from over the edge of the world. To make her a story with an ending.

He went to the hallway cupboard to get his rucksack. He packed quickly, not needing much.

14

Kenny considered parking the Combi in an out-of-town lay-by; there were plenty between Bristol and Bath. But locals of his generation well remembered what happened to unwary New Age travellers round this time of year — hippies with dirty dreadlocks and skinny dogs, who stopped their vans and buses on private land. Kenny didn't want to be dragged from the back of the Combi, still half asleep, then kicked unconscious in the bushes.

So he drove to a campsite on the outskirts of town. According to its website, it had free Wifi, a bar and an award-winning toilet block — although what award wasn't specified.

By the time he'd parked and paid his deposit, it was dusk. He sat near the camp bar, alone on a bench alongside a trout stream. He was annoyed by a swirl of midges. Around him sat foreign students, dressed like Kenny in cargo shorts and walking sandals. There were families on camping trips, and elderly tourists with hired Winnebagos.

Kenny sipped from a pint of lager with a lemonade top, browsing the internet on his iPhone.

The Jonathan Reese he was looking for didn't have a page on any social networking site of which Kenny was aware. There were other Jonathan Reeses out there, other faces. But none of them was the Jonathan Reese he was looking for.

By Googling the name, however, Kenny stumbled across a website dedicated to Callie Reese.

He'd avoided looking for her — she wasn't the point of this search. But there she was anyway. Jonathan's name had brought her to him.

The sun was going down, the voices around him grew low and intimate and the rich smell of England rose from the land; grass and soil and oak and ash and lager.

On the website — whereiscallie.com — there were posted perhaps a dozen portraits. Jonathan, it appeared, was a talented photographer.

Here she was, captured at the breakfast table, laughing. And here she was, at the front door, in some kind of business suit. Here she was on holiday, a garland of flowers around her neck, her skin glistening. And here she was, in pensive close-up, gazing out of a rainy window.

Zooming in on this image, Kenny could see

the laugh-lines at the corners of her mouth: the lighting had made them more pronounced. It had done the same to the wrinkles at the corners of her eyes.

To him, these wrinkles were like cracks in the varnish of an old painting; he could see only the flawlessness beneath.

Zooming out again, he saw that in the bottom corner of the frame was a spray of wild flowers. They were reflected in the curve of her cornea.

She was no longer the snatched, blurry snapshot he'd seen in the newspaper reports. Here, her image was crisp and unfaded because on the internet there was no time, just infinite, discontinuous moments like fragments of a reflected face in shards of a broken mirror.

The site had been set up by Jonathan Reese. Its purpose was to request information that might lead to Callie's return.

The likelihood of her death was not so much as hinted at, although its unspoken possibility had lent a strange gravity to every page and every image.

The website requested information, but gave little away. It could be contacted via an impersonal email address. Comments were disabled. Kenny didn't like to imagine what kind of mind visited websites like this, what terrible things they would type and leave for ever, if permitted.

Returning to the home page, he noted that the site hadn't been updated for more than a year.

Something opened in his chest. It was grief and anger that this should be Callie Barton's marker — just an internet page which said: here she is, laughing. And here she is, looking out of a rainy window. And here she is on holiday.

It never said: this is the position she slept in; or this is how she stood when she cleaned her teeth; or this is how she laughed when she was watching her favourite TV show, or this was her brand of tampons. It just said: this is her face. And here was that face, like an unvisited and untended grave. She was an effigy. Not even a portrait.

Kenny recalled her playing elastics, how she and Isabel would be breathless and dishevelled as they folded the rope of knotted elastic bands away and hurried back to class.

He recalled how she'd hook her ankle round his under the desk, and how the tip of her tongue peeped from the corner of her mouth when she concentrated on long division or grammar, her weakest subjects.

Kenny wondered if there was anyone left in

the world who knew and cared what Callie Barton's weakest subjects had been.

* * *

He paid a visit to the award-winning toilet block. It was very clean, well lit and bracingly tangy with pine-scented chemical cleaner. Then he wandered back to the Combi.

He took off his shorts and socks and slithered into a sleeping bag. With a bedroll beneath him, it wasn't a bad way to sleep. He could hear the people outside, coming and going.

Shortly before 10 p.m., Pat called. 'Where are you, Sunny Jim?'

'At home.'

'No you're not.'

'No, I'm not. How'd you know?'

'Because I'm at your house.'

'Ah.'

'I came to see you. I'm there now, looking in the window. It's all dark.'

'I might've been asleep.'

'I'm a trained detective. So I instantly noted the absence of your huge, bright orange Volkswagen van.'

'Right.'

'So where are you?'

'Stonehenge.'

'Stonehenge? Why?'

'I wanted to see it. Y'know. Have a look, while I had the chance. I had a few beers, so I settled down for the night.'

'In the van?'

'It's been a long time since I did that. I miss it. Mary and me, we used to drive to the beach, down in Devon, on a Friday night. We'd wake up early on Saturday morning and smell the sea. And nobody else would be up yet. We'd be all bleary and hot. So we'd run into the sea, starkers. Naked as the day.'

'I bet that woke you up.'

'Like you wouldn't believe. We'd run back to the van, all goose-bumpy. And no matter how hard you tried, there'd always be sand in the towels. We'd make breakfast on this little Primus stove we had. And the first oldies would start to come along.'

'Because the old don't sleep.'

'Yep. They'd be walking their dogs on the beach. Golden retrievers and what have you.'

He shut up for a minute, thinking about it.

Pat said: 'Have you spoken to Mary?'

'No.'

'She's worried about you.'

'Have *you* spoken to her?'

'Depends what you mean by 'spoken'?'

'I mean, did you tell her? About me.'

'It's not my place. But she knows

something's wrong.'

'I know she does.'

'So tell her.'

'When the time's right.'

'When will that be?'

'I don't know.'

There was a pause, then Pat said: 'When you're gone, she'll still be here. Don't leave her thinking she let you down. Because it's not a nice thing — to think you weren't there when you were needed by someone you love.'

Kenny was going to say: 'Okay', but Pat had hung up on him.

He began tapping out a text to Mary. Then he deleted it and turned off the phone and plugged it into the cigarette lighter to recharge. He swallowed a number of pills, curled up on the bedroll and went to sleep.

* * *

In the stillness of the campsite not long after dawn, as mist rose from the trout stream, Kenny scuttled to the toilet block to have a shower. He shaved barefoot with a towel round his waist, then wandered back to the Combi in flip-flops.

He put on some deodorant and his cargo shorts, his walking sandals and a clean T-shirt, and was the first for breakfast.

He accessed the internet while he waited.

According to the online satellite photographs, the Kennet and Avon Canal ran round the back of Coney Lane. A footpath followed the canal. A small area of urban woodland acted as a screen between garden fences and towpath.

After breakfast, he packed his rucksack with a bottle of water and a crowbar he took from the Combi's wheel-changing kit.

He put on his baseball cap and sunglasses, slapped on some factor 15 — as much to smell right, as anything else — and went to do it.

15

As he set off, the campsite was waking all around him. The smell of bacon, sounds of unzipping tents, people in flip-flops carrying wash-bags to the toilet block.

He found the tree-shaded canal path and followed it for two miles. He was ignored by the fishermen — transfixed, retired men.

It wasn't yet 9 a.m. when he found the point where the canal path backed on to Coney Lane.

He reversed, headed back the way he'd come, turned on to a brambly path. At length, it became an alley between high-walled gardens. Finally, it gave on to the streets of suburban Bath.

The area was made up of four-storey Victorian terraces in Bath stone, most of them converted into flats lived in by young professional couples, house-sharers, some students.

Larger, detached houses backed on to the canal. They were no longer grand; weeds grew from cracks in the walls and garden paths. Number 25 Coney Lane was typical of them, right down to its small, untidy front garden.

Callie Barton had lived here.

Kenny tried to imagine her standing in that window, looking out.

He wanted to walk to the door. But he didn't.

Instead, he stood in view of the house and dialled the mobile phone number of Bath Garden Landscapes.

It rang six times. Then he heard: 'Landscapes. Jonathan speaking.'

Kenny almost let out a noise, but held it in and said: 'Hi there. I'm calling from Churchill Drive.'

'I know Churchill Drive, yeah. Out by the Feeder.'

'That's the one.'

'So what can I do you for?'

'I'm looking for a quote. We've had some plans drawn up. If I dropped them round, could you maybe have a look at the size of the job . . . ?'

'I'm afraid we don't give quotes from plans.'

'I'm just talking ballpark. Trying to get my budget worked out.'

'Well, yeah. I could certainly have a look, get back to you. View the actual property next week?'

'That would be perfect,' said Kenny. 'Where can I drop the plans?'

'You could pop them in the post. But if you're in town, I'm on site for the rest of the day. You could drop them round, if you like.'

'I wouldn't be able to make it until, say, four thirty.'

'That's fine. We'll be here all day.'

'Give me the address,' said Kenny. 'I'll jot it down.'

* * *

Kenny almost wished he really did have some plans for a house on Churchill Drive; he'd have liked to meet Jonathan Reese while strengthened by this fantasy of being someone else, another man with another life.

But there were no architectural plans and there was no house out by the Feeder. And now Kenny knew that Jonathan wouldn't be home for the rest of the day.

He returned to the canal path, sure of his bearings now, and counted houses again. The garden fences were just visible through a copse of spindly silver birch and hazel which formed a barrier between gardens walls and the public footway.

When Kenny had counted to the correct house he stopped, removed his rucksack and took out the bottle of mineral water. He used the few seconds it took to slake his thirst to check out the towpath, left and right. No one was around.

He stepped into the undergrowth, moving through the low, whipping branches. It made him recall being a child — what it had been like to know secret places.

The rear garden of Number 25 had a wooden gate. Its brick wall stood higher than Kenny's head, tumbling with loops of an ancient creeping vine. Nettles overflowed in the purple shadows.

Kenny knew from the online map that behind this wall a long, narrow garden gave on to what looked like a conservatory. The conservatory gave access to the house.

The gate was secured with a tarnished brass padlock, but the hasp to which the padlock attached was rusted, set into wood that was halfway to rot.

Kenny applied the crowbar to the hasp. The old damp wood gave with little effort and all but silently.

Even so, Kenny decided to wait, squatting in the shadow of the wall. Should he be seen now, there was no lie that could be told about what he was going to do next.

A cold part of him — this new part, the avenger of Callie Barton — didn't care. He opened the garden gate and stepped through.

It took some self-control, but he ambled

along the mature, unkempt garden as if it were a public footpath until he reached a paved sun-deck.

There was no point trying the kitchen door, so he went to the sash windows that looked into the long sitting room. He peeked inside.

The way the sun reflected on the glass, he could barely see anything, not until he had his nose pressed to the pane. He was so close his quick breath made blooms of condensation, quickly fading.

He was seeing the room through the darkness cast by the outline of his own face.

He saw furniture that perhaps a decade ago might have been considered chic but was now scuffed and scratched.

Then he heard a noise.

It might have been one of the old hazel trees groaning in the rising heat of the day, or it might have been a curious neighbour.

Kenny jammed the crowbar into the window frame and levered.

Nothing happened, so he tried again, pushing harder. And the brass bolt holding the window shut began to give.

Kenny levered again, as hard as he could. The bolt creaked and finally gave. Kenny raised the window.

Doing that set off the burglar alarm.

It was shocking in the fly-buzzed silence, in this long, mature back garden halfway between a canal and a suburban road; a sudden, terrified shrieking, as if the house itself were calling out in terror.

Kenny knew he could run away, and probably would not be caught. But he also knew that, if he ran away now, he'd never have the courage to come back.

So he raised the window another few inches and clambered into the house. Here, the shrieking was even louder and more hysterical.

He stood in the hallway, breathing heavily — the crowbar in his fist — estimating how quickly he could expect the police to respond.

Because Jonathan Reese's alarm had been tripped in the morning, they'd probably consider it accidental — set off by a rat or a magpie.

If not, the house could have been penetrated by a wandering, opportunistic junkie who'd have scarpered the moment the alarm went off, having stuffed a couple of medium-value items into a sports bag.

More likely still: the neighbours would sit round bleating about the noise until one of them cracked and called Jonathan to come home and sort it out.

Kenny reckoned he had some time.

He went upstairs, only half-conscious of the alarm now.

He looked in the upstairs rooms.

The first bedroom he tried was set up to be a home office — a library, really, complete with a leather and chrome chair, much used. On the shelves were illustrated books on home movie making, local history, gardening and design; cook books by Jamie Oliver and Gordon Ramsey and Nigella Lawson.

A Hewlett Packard computer sat on a smoked glass desk, surrounded by piled-up paper invoices and stock orders. Jonathan used interesting pebbles as paperweights; first polished to a high shine, now left to grow dusty.

A smaller bedroom was empty. Kenny stood in the doorway for a long time, looking at it. Pale walls, bare floorboards, a sash window overlooking the garden.

Its emptiness spooked him. He closed the door on it.

In one corner of the landing was propped a length of dowelling topped with a brass hook. Kenny lifted and examined it, wondered what it was. Then he put it back in the corner and took a look at the main bedroom.

There was a double bed in there. A double wardrobe.

Kenny went to the wardrobe. It was full of

men's clothing. Kenny thought about the empty room next door, and realized what the brass hook on the end of the dowelling was for.

He stepped on to the landing, looking up. There, in the ceiling, was a metal eyelet. It had been painted to match its surroundings.

Kenny took the length of dowelling and worked the brass hook into the eyelet. Then he yanked downwards — and the hatch that gave on to the attic opened with a squeal of angle brackets and a shudder of paint flakes.

Kenny returned the dowelling to its corner, pulled down the folding ladder and climbed into the attic.

It was hot and airless. Narrow sunbeams, twisting with dust, shone at acute angles through tiny fissures in the woodwork. Kenny sneezed three times.

The attic was half full with a random-looking collection of stuff — a blue suitcase with scuffed corners, a lava lamp on its side, a tea chest, a box of books, an exercise bike.

In the far corner, piled into a wide-based pyramid, were stacked perhaps a dozen identical cardboard boxes, each sealed with parcel tape.

Kenny knew the kind of boxes — they hadn't been blagged from a corner shop or a supermarket; they'd been bought, flat-packed, at an out-of-town stationers, and assembled downstairs.

They'd been packed and sealed on the same day, then moved to the attic.

Kenny used his car keys to slit the tape and opened one of the boxes.

It contained a woman's clothing.

He took out a blouse — white, diaphanous and summery. It had no human smell, no trace of perfume, but rather the stale biscuity scent of cardboard box and hot attic. He lay it down. From the box he took some T-shirts and two fleeces in dark green and luminous pink.

Another box was full of shoes: high-heels, flip-flops, strappy sandals, court shoes. Most of the inner soles were darkened with the imprint of a woman's heel.

A third box was full of trinkets. He removed a velveteen jewellery box, inside which were some thin silver chains, some rings. One of them was a Victorian mourning ring: an amber lozenge set in silver. Between the amber lozenge and the blackening silver was pressed a curl of human hair.

Kenny wondered at the ring, knowing the hair had been snipped from a corpse, then worn on a pale finger as a reminder of lost love.

But how had it come through time to be here, in a cardboard box, in this attic?

He looked at the ring for a long time.

He was still looking at it when he heard the front door slam.

16

Kenny had become so accustomed to the endless panic of the alarm that it had become no more than background noise — like the hullabaloo of traffic through the windows of an inner-city flat. So he heard the door slam as if in a silent house.

Hearing it, he became aware of the alarm again — at once, it was all he could hear, the unrestrained screaming of this violated house.

He scurried over to grab the loop of rope and hauled up the attic stairs, closing the hatch just as the alarm cut off.

It left in its wake a silence so profound that Kenny feared to move in case it shattered.

* * *

He put an ear to a narrow gap in the frame of the hatch. There were voices downstairs: two men.

Then the tread of feet on the stairs.

Through the gap in the frame, Kenny saw a quick blur of dark hair. The man ducked into his office, probably to confirm the computer was there.

The second man came upstairs, his tread marking him out as bigger and heavier than the first. 'They've done your window, mate — out back, overlooking the garden. Got in that way.'

'Fuck a fucking duck,' said Jonathan Reese.

'Most probably he was a Rupert,' said the second man. 'Half the junkies round here are Ruperts. The toerag that did over my place wasn't a Rupert. He was a chav. He shat on the carpet; a great big curler. I nearly threw up. To this day, I can't face a Cumberland sausage.'

'Right. Thanks for that, Ollie.'

Jonathan hit the bathroom light and the extractor fan came on. Kenny heard him urinating, marking his territory. Then a flush being pulled.

Kenny strained to hear as Jonathan followed Ollie back downstairs and phoned the police. It took some time, and Jonathan grew short tempered. Then he hung up and told Ollie: 'Apparently they'll be round this evening between six and eight thirty.'

'You're a high-priority case, then.'

'Whatever.'

'Fuck's sake.'

'Look, I'll be okay here. You get back on site. Dunwoody gives you grief, explain what happened.'

'What'll you do?'

'Have a cup of tea. Watch *Judge Judy*. Do some paperwork, invoicing. Tax. Wait for Plod. Get out a glazier to fix the window.'

'I could hang around.'

'Nah . . . you shoot off, mate. Have a look at that bit of the path, the bit running up behind the pond. And get on to Nicholson's about the fencing.'

'You sure you're all right?'

'Yep.'

'Give me a bell if you need to.'

'All right. Off you fuck then. Back to work.'

There was the sound of cordial laughter. The front door closing.

Then the sounds of a man believing himself to be alone, taking a deep breath in his unoccupied hallway.

Then walking upstairs, to his office.

Through the gap in the frame, Kenny watched the blur of Jonathan's head as he passed below.

From the office came a sequence of small, familiar noises: a mouse being jiggled to waken a sleeping computer; the weight of a man settling into an office chair; the whine of a computer's cooling fan kicking into life, rapid tapping on a keyboard.

* * *

Kenny glanced at the pyramid of boxes which held fleeces and blouses maintaining no trace of human scent, and shoes etched with a dark stain of a woman's heel.

Then he lay with his eyes open and waited. He was a wraith in the attic, a recording demon, tabulating Jonathan's life, finding him wanting.

17

Kenny listened as Jonathan Reese made business calls — to suppliers, to Ollie, to various glaziers, to a couple of clients.

After 4 p.m., when he'd finished the business calls and found a twenty-four-hour glazier willing to come out after teatime, he seemed to be at a loose end.

He walked round the house for a bit. Kenny heard him checking the windows and singing a song under his breath — 'Celebrate!' by Kool and the Gang. Earlier, it had been on the radio and must have snagged in his head, the way some songs do.

He stood in the hallway, dialling a number, then tutted. He hesitated, then said: 'Babe, it's me. Half four, just about. Listen, I'm not sure I'll make it round tonight. Had a bit of a weird day, to be honest. Anyway, sorry. Hope everything's okay. Give us a call when you can. Love you. Bye.'

After that, he returned to the office.

Kenny could hear small-arms gunfire, the screams of the dying, the roar of tanks as Jonathan played some kind of war game.

Sometime after five fifteen, Jonathan gave

up on the game and wandered away from the office.

Halfway down the stairs, his phone rang. He said, 'Babe! How you doing?' and sat down on the stairs.

By adjusting his head and squinting through the crack in the frame, Kenny could just about see Jonathan's hand as it tugged and twisted at the weave of the seagrass carpet. He heard Jonathan say: 'No, nothing really bad. Nothing like that. The house got broken into.'

Jonathan spoke for ten minutes — *No, they didn't take anything. Yeah, right, believe it when I see it* — before hanging up.

He stayed sitting on the stairs for a long time, elbows on his knees. He was still sitting there when the police arrived.

⋆ ⋆ ⋆

As the two police officers — one male, one female — made their cursory inspection of the house, Kenny lay motionless as the dead.

Jonathan tailed the officers. 'So the alarm goes off . . .'

'It's not monitored?'

'It used to be. But forty-five quid a month? Anyway. My neighbours give me a call and I'm round as soon as I can. But he's gone before I get back. What're the chances of catching him?'

The female officer said: 'Not high, I'm afraid.'

Kenny knew that certain police officers affected a contemptuous demeanour when investigating crimes they considered a petty irritation. But there was something else in this officer's voice, a chilly bluntness that made Kenny wonder if she and Jonathan had perhaps met before, under different circumstances: perhaps she'd been to this address some years ago. Perhaps she'd stood in the kitchen while Scenes of Crime Officers in white paper bunny suits and latex gloves hunted out blood-splatter or other indications of violent disagreement. Or perhaps she'd stood guard behind a perimeter while, out back, SOCO fingertip-searched the long garden.

In the end, Jonathan gave up seeking to ingratiate himself. He sighed and said: 'So what do I do next?'

'Think about fitting sturdier locks to the windows, automatic lights.'

'It happened at nine o'clock in the morning.'

'Perhaps buy a dog.'

'And this is official police policy, is it? Buy a dog.'

'Burglars don't like dogs. What can I say?'

'Well, thanks for the advice.'

'No problem. Evening, sir.'

'Yeah, yeah. See you later.'
Jonathan closed the door.

* * *

Shortly before 8 p.m., the glazier arrived. He was there for three-quarters of an hour, cleaning and measuring up.

He and Jonathan discussed the number of burglaries in the area — they discussed absurdly lenient prison sentences handed out to repeat offenders and political correctness gone mad. They agreed to bring back the short, sharp shock, National Service and possibly hanging. Then the glazier gave Jonathan a quote for the job, including the cost of making a new oak frame for the sash window.

The glazier hammered at something, probably fixing a square of plywood to the broken window frame. Then he was gone, too, and the house was silent.

Jonathan drew the curtains and double-locked all the doors. Then he trudged upstairs, to the office.

* * *

Kenny heard him, sitting there, operating the mouse. Around nine, Jonathan's phone rang. He ignored it.

The beams of sunlight lancing the attic were the colour of barley; outside, the mid-summer sun was beginning to set.

Jonathan's phone rang again at nine thirty. He continued to ignore it.

By now, there were other sounds.

They were coming from the computer speakers: a loud camcorder hiss, over which Kenny could hear a woman's voice — low moaning and rapid breathing. A muttered word. A grunt.

'Come on,' said Jonathan, but not the real Jonathan; it was the Jonathan on screen, on the computer.

At this insistence, the woman's cries progressed in frequency and pitch.

'Come on,' said Jonathan. Muttered through his teeth, over the camcorder hiss.

The office chair creaked as the real Jonathan sat back.

'There you are,' said Jonathan, on screen. 'There you are. There you are.'

Kenny listened to the creaks of Jonathan masturbating. They were timed with the low exclamations of the woman reaching orgasm.

Jonathan spat God's name through gritted teeth.

There followed a moment of near-silence.

Then Jonathan stood from his chair, muttering.

Clutching his unbuttoned jeans in one hand, he waddled from the office to the bathroom.

The taps ran, then stopped.

* * *

Kenny turned to lie on his back. He saw the shafts of sunlight, pale rose now, advancing from a much lower angle. Night was coming, and he was trapped in this attic while Jonathan stood a few feet away, washing the semen from his thighs and belly.

Kenny smelled distant, burning tyres. It was an oddly summery smell.

But there were no burning tyres.

The left side of Kenny's face went cold. His heel kicked at the attic floor once, twice, three times, like a drummer counting in a song. Then Kenny went into seizure.

His teeth clenched. His mouth frothed. His body beat a tattoo on the attic floor, three feet above Jonathan's head.

* * *

The seizure ended. Below Kenny, there was a hush.

From somewhere inside it, Jonathan said: 'Hello?'

18

Kenny lay still.

Downstairs, Jonathan was taking the length of dowelling from the corner. His breathing was shallow and rapid.

Kenny heard the hook scraping then engaging the eyelet that lowered the attic hatch.

He scuttled like a rat to the furthest, darkest corner.

The boxes here were older — slightly damp, connected to the eaves by cobwebs grown pearly grey with dust, ornate with insect husks.

What sound he made was veiled by the grating protest of the attic hatch — and then by the clatter of the ladder being unfolded.

Kenny squatted heel to haunch in the spidery shadows, watching as the attic hatch became an oblong of electric light. He realized how dark it had become.

Across that yellow oblong passed a flicker of shadow that was Jonathan beginning to climb the ladder.

Kenny hunkered lower, his urine-wet shorts clinging to his thighs. Cobwebs caught in his hair.

Jonathan entered the attic holding a three-cell torch — a foot-long tube of battery-weighted aluminium. He swept the attic with its beam; it angled as it moved over the boxes, the suitcase, the exercise bike, then straightened and widened into the corners.

It passed over a woman's shoe.

It stopped.

Jonathan was a silhouette behind the torch's bright eye, staring at the shoe.

Then he probed the corners of the attic with the brisk, shaky beam. 'Hello?'

Watching him through a narrow gap in the boxes, Kenny was almost tempted to reply — to just stand up, wave, say hello and get it over with.

Perhaps in his shock, Jonathan would take a step backwards and tumble down the hatch, breaking his neck on the way down.

Then Kenny could wait until it was late and let himself out the back door and scurry down the long, night-cool garden, concealed by the shadows of those mature trees. He could walk through the garden gate and scramble through the thicket of birch and hazel, pale in the night, and tramp along the canal towpath until he reached the trout stream.

He could stroll, half-noticed at best, to the

Combi. He could drive away and be home in an hour.

But he was rigid with uncertainty, worried about the luminosity of his white hair and teeth and eyes.

Jonathan stood equally undecided, his dark form like a lighthouse behind the torch beam, saying once again: 'Hello?'

He wasn't scared of burglars. If that had been the case, he'd have backed away from the attic and dialled 999.

He'd been frightened by the angry knocking on the ceiling. And then shocked to the bone by that single, upended shoe — lying where it did not belong and should not be.

Then the doorbell rang.

It jolted Kenny such that he almost cried out. But any sound he made was covered by Jonathan's bolt of fright. He shouted something and his hand flew to his chest, as if he feared his heart might stop.

The doorbell rang again — a commonplace sound now. Jonathan muttered, 'Fuck me' in an unselfconscious, irritated way. Not the voice of a man who believed himself to be overheard.

He shone the torch round the attic once more, then hurried down the ladder. Kenny heard him bounding downstairs, two or three at a time, then opening the front door.

A woman saying: 'Can I come in, then?'

'I didn't think you were coming over.'

'You sounded funny.'

'Did I? Hey, come up here a minute. Have a look at this.'

'At what?'

'Up here.'

He hurried her upstairs. She protested all the way.

Kenny burrowed himself further into the corner, lifting his jacket to cover his white hair and curling like a hedgehog on the floor.

Two people climbed the ladder now — Jonathan, followed by the woman saying: 'So what was it?'

'I don't know. That's the point.'

'But what did it sound like?'

'I don't know. Banging.'

'What sort of banging?'

'Just banging.'

'It was probably a bird.'

'Then it was a big bird — a fucking ostrich or something.'

'We had this bird trapped in our attic, once. When I was little. They panic, birds — when they can't find a way out. They make a lot of noise.'

'I didn't see a bird.'

'It must've got out.'

‘I don’t even know how it got in.’

‘You need to call out a roofer, get him to have a look. Or it could be rats.’

‘But the shoe.’

‘What shoe?’

Jonathan moved to her shoulder, saying, ‘That shoe.’

She was holding the torch and he moved her wrist until its beam fell like a spotlight on the shoe.

‘What about it?’

‘It’s one of hers.’

She tutted and stepped forward to pick up the shoe. Kenny could smell her, a burst of bright perfume in this musty place. She shone the torch across the pyramid of boxes, then reached out to touch one of them.

‘You left the box unsealed.’

‘No, I didn’t.’

‘You must have. Look.’

She lifted a flap to show him the box was open.

Jonathan said, ‘It wasn’t like that before.’

‘So what are you saying? Someone came up here, did some break-dancing, left a shoe on the floor?’

‘No.’

‘Then what?’

‘I don’t know. All I know, last time I came up here . . . ’

'And when was that?'

'Ages ago. Years ago. Before we met. Way before.'

She waited, then said: 'It must've fallen out of the box when you brought it up here.'

'The boxes were sealed.'

'So what are you saying?'

'I don't know.'

'Christ, Jon.'

'Christ what?'

'It's a shoe. What do you want me to say?'

'There was banging.'

'It was birds, it was rats, it was next door's kids banging on their attic windows. I don't know what it was. I do know it wasn't the Magical Flip-Flop Thief.'

She let the torch beam relax so that it illuminated her feet. Kenny could see her shoes.

She sighed, and in a much quieter voice said: 'Why do you keep her things anyway? Are you waiting for her to come back, take up where you left off?'

'No.'

She muttered something that might have been *yeah, right* and climbed back down to the landing.

Jonathan hung around for a moment, gazing into the darkness. Then he followed her.

* * *

On the landing, Jonathan was irritated, safe under the bright electric light. He said, 'How do you think it would've looked, if I'd thrown away her stuff? What sort of message do you think that would've sent?'

'I'm not saying then. I'm saying now.'

'Fine.'

'So why don't you do it?'

'Oh, come on, Becks.'

'Is she coming home?'

'No!'

'Then why keep her stuff?'

'It's no big secret, and no big deal. Did you think I was keeping, like, a shrine?'

'That's a bit what it looks like, yeah.'

'Hey, come on. Don't go.'

'I think I'd better.'

'Don't. Please. Come on.'

'I'll call you tomorrow.'

'Look, Becks. I just don't think about it. I mean, I know that stuff's up there, but it's not like I think about it. Or her. Or whatever. I just don't think about it — I don't want to think about it.'

She turned on the stair. The bannister creaked. Jonathan said, 'Stay. Come on. This is silly.'

'Are you waiting for her to come back?'

'No.'

'I'm not sure that's true.'

'This has got nothing to do with her! This is ridiculous!'

'You hear a pigeon in the attic and you see a shoe you dropped and have a full-blown episode. And I'm the one being ridiculous?'

'Who's having an episode? I'm not having an episode.'

'You're having an episode.'

'For fuck's sake. I'm a bit irritated, yeah. I'm a bit wound up. I got burgled, I've got a marching band yomping round my attic. But I'm not having an episode. This is me, not having an episode. Look. No episode.'

The stairs creaked again as she softened.

She joined him on the landing, gave him a cuddle, told him: 'You need to move.'

'I know.'

'So why don't you?'

'Dunno. Back then — when it all happened — I couldn't. It would've looked bad. So I had to stay put.'

'And now?'

'And now I can't afford it.'

'Come here.' She kissed him. 'Poor baby.'

'Don't laugh.'

'I'm not laughing.'

She sat down, her back to the bannister. He sat down next to her. They held hands.

She said, 'My place is nice. Smaller, but nice.'

'I know.'

'Then move in.'

'I can't.'

'Why not?'

'Just can't.'

She let go his hand. She stood, went downstairs. Jonathan lingered on the landing as if trapped there, but eventually he followed.

* * *

When Jonathan and Becks came to bed, Jonathan pushed the ladder inside the attic as if it were a prolapse.

They murmured in bed for another half an hour, intimate but tired, in no mood for sex.

Soon enough, Jonathan was asleep. Kenny could hear him softly snoring.

But he couldn't believe that Becks was asleep.

He imagined that she lay there with her eyes pinned to the ceiling — looking through it, seeing Kenny all shrouded in cobwebs, an abandoned fairground for mice and spiders.

Just after 2 a.m., he heard her get out of bed and creep out of the bedroom.

He sensed she was beneath the hatch. Just stood there, staring up at it. Then he heard her creep back to bed.

19

In the morning, Jonathan and Becks were subdued, taking it in turns to shower, Becks first.

She made coffee and toast while Jonathan showered. She kissed him goodbye while he was still wrapped in his towel.

Ten minutes later Jonathan left the house, too. He checked all the windows and double-locked the doors.

* * *

For an hour, Kenny stayed hidden behind the boxes in the corner. Being up there was like being a spider.

Eventually, he straightened. His back and his legs sent out bright bolts of pain. Stiff, he clambered over the boxes and stood in the half-light, wiping the worst of the cobwebs from his hair and clothes.

He opened the hatch and climbed down into the house which — glimpsed only briefly the day before — now seemed familiar and homey.

Kenny went to the bathroom. He gargled

with mouthwash, then finger-cleaned his teeth with a dab of toothpaste. He poked his head into the shower and ran the water over his head to get rid of the cobwebs.

He put his T-shirt back on, hung up the towel and went down to the kitchen.

He rinsed out a coffee cup that sat upended on the drainer, filling it with cold water. Before he could drink, his phone rang. It was Mary.

He said, 'Hey, Mary.'

'Hey, you. Where are you?'

'Bath.'

'Bath? You hate Bath.'

'Not Bath, really. I'm at a campsite. They've got these amazing toilet facilities.'

'You've come up in the world. Last time I went camping with you, I had to poo in a bush.'

'I don't remember that.'

'I do. So — you coming home?'

He was looking out of the kitchen window, down the long garden.

Mary said: 'Are you there?'

'Yeah, I'm here.'

'What's wrong?'

'Nothing.'

'Something's wrong. Pat thinks so, too.'

'Have you been talking to Pat?'

'Yeah.'

'You can't stand her.'

'She's an old cow, but she's your friend.'

'Am I not allowed to go away for a couple of days?'

'Not when you've been acting so weird.'

'Have I been acting weird?'

'Yep.'

'Well, I'm coming home today. I'll pop in and see you.'

'Good. When?'

'This afternoon?'

'Promise?'

'Absolutely.'

'I love you.'

'I love you too.'

He hung up and put the phone away, then went upstairs to Jonathan's office.

He sat in the office chair and hit a key. Jonathan's screensaver dissolved — revealing a Text Entry field which required a password.

Kenny ran his hands underneath the desk and found nothing.

He went through the drawers; they were tidy and organized and contained nothing he was looking for.

He went through the books on the shelf, flicking through them one by one, page by page. He'd gone through perhaps twenty-five before he opened the RHS *A-Z Encyclopedia of Garden Plants*. Inside the dust-jacket he found a folded, printed sheet of A4.

Listed on it were a number of Jonathan's usernames and passwords. The uppermost password was Jonathan's administrator log-in. Kenny entered it, then flicked through Jonathan's emails. Most of them were work-related and quickly became tedious.

Much of Jonathan's communication with Becks, Kenny supposed, would be via text message — that was the modern lovers' preferred means of correspondence.

He ran a quick search on Callie's name, but found nothing. And anyway, he knew what he'd come to find.

Jonathan had hidden the home movies inside private folders, but anyone who knew what he was looking for wouldn't be long in finding them — and Kenny spent a lot of time alone, with a computer, manipulating scanned images and managing complex file structures. He found the videos after only a cursory search, looking not by file name but file type, searching for all files ending WMV.

Here were the videos of Callie Barton. Callie Reese. Eight of them in all, each backed up with a duplicate marked 'safe–copy'.

In the first of them, Callie was masturbating in the bath. It was a different bath in a different house. Two hands moving between her legs; her breasts glistening with water.

Jonathan was filming her from the doorway; all Kenny could hear was the hiss of the camcorder and Jonathan's breathing, the occasional word he muttered to her.

Kenny skipped to the third film. Here she was in a hotel room, lying on the bed wearing nothing but a pair of shoes, one of the pairs Kenny had found in the box upstairs. She lifted her legs and locked her ankles behind Jonathan's back, grabbing the bedstead with both hands and arching her spine. Her muscles grew taut, her hair was sweated flat to her brow.

Kenny looked at five of the eight films. Callie's hair got longer, got shorter. He never heard her voice, just her shy giggles and sometimes a little profane muttering.

She was on her knees in an evening dress that had been yanked down to expose her breasts and she was moaning, moving towards orgasm.

Jonathan was saying *there you are, there you are*. Urging her on.

There you are. There you are.

She was face down on the bed in another hotel room — a foreign hotel. When Jonathan lifted the camcorder and walked away, she looked at the lens, frozen for an instant.

Kenny's penis shrivelled; it seemed to

burrow up and into him, as it did sometimes when he was very, very cold.

⋆ ⋆ ⋆

He sat with his head in his hands and tried to conjure up that elastics-playing little girl in her white knee socks, the girl missing her front teeth, the girl who'd secretly hooked her ankle round his under the desk. Instead, he saw a woman's ankles locking round a man's spine, the mechanical undulation of her hips. Not bruised knees but the badger-stripe of pubic hair.

He put the computer to sleep and replaced the passwords in the dust-jacket of the gardening book.

He went downstairs and let himself out the back door. He walked down that mature garden.

Trapped in the attic, he'd missed the fresh air. But the air out here didn't taste fresh; it tasted of mulch and rot, the sour reek of ivy and crumbling fence-wood. Along the tow-path, there was only scum and stagnant water.

He walked until he found the trout stream and followed it to the campsite.

It was a warm day, threatening rain. The campsite was almost empty, but dotted with red tents and blue tents and white Oldsmobiles.

In the far corner, under a hazel tree, was Kenny's VW Combi — bright orange, rusty round the rims, faithful.

He opened the door, got in, closed the Paisley curtains and lay on the foam mattress in the baked-in-heat of the summer: the good, familiar smells of a life to which he could never return.

He curled up, trying to make the knowledge of what he had to do next go away. But it wouldn't go away, and it was still there when he woke, waiting for him.

20

Kenny left the campsite again at teatime, just as it was reaching its most relaxed and convivial.

He drove the Combi to the suburbs, pulling over once or twice to access Google Maps. He drove round until he found what he believed to be the optimum street, given what he had to work with.

After parking there was a lot of time to kill so he went for an exploratory wander, during which he came across a yellow skip. Inside the skip, along with a great deal of builder's waste, was half a brick. He picked it up, examined it, and walked on, clutching the brick loosely in his hand.

He kept walking. Loitering might draw attention to him — to this youngish man with hair so white it seemed to glow in the twilight.

Kenny took a circular route past the chip shops and the curry houses and the corner shops and the shut-down newsagents. His eyesight was bright and true; the darkness was not really darkness, just a deep summer purple.

After midnight, he walked to Number 25 Coney Lane.

He stopped across the road, facing it, bouncing the half-brick in his hand like a cricket ball. Then he pitched it through Jonathan Reese's living-room window.

The noise was brilliant and urgent, shattered glass cascading like a waterfall; Kenny imagined it echoing over the city, waking everyone in their safe beds.

He wanted to call something, to scream an obscenity. But the words jammed in his throat as Jonathan pulled back the curtain and stood at the living-room window.

He saw Kenny.

There was a shock of connection.

Then Jonathan moved. Kenny watched the weird, angular shadows he cast as he hurried into his shoes.

He heard Jonathan thundering down the hallway, fumbling the chain from the latch, opening the front door.

He waited until Jonathan came outside and shouted: 'Oi!'

Then Kenny ran — not too fast at first. Not until he knew for sure that Jonathan was following.

* * *

Jonathan's footfalls echoed from the pavements and the low garden walls as he chased Kenny to the dark end of the street.

Kenny rounded the corner and stopped.

This road was straight and long, edged on both sides with parked cars. At the far end it crossed a main road, brightly lit, still busy enough with traffic.

There were gardens to hide in and passages between houses, shadowy back gardens. Behind him, a left turn would lead him to the local train station — it was closed; chained and bolted for the night. There were many places to hide.

But Kenny didn't hide. He pushed on, nursing a stitch, until he reached the Combi.

He stepped between the front grille of the Combi and the boot of the Vauxhall Astra parked in front of it. He rummaged until he found the crowbar where he'd left it, tucked behind the front wheel.

Then he flattened his spine to the cold metal and waited. His breathing was too loud, rasping and painful.

He made a promise to himself: if Jonathan had given up and gone home, then Kenny would give up, too.

But then Jonathan passed by, having slowed his sprint to a laboured jog.

Kenny stepped out from his hiding place,

lifting the crowbar high, bringing it down.

Jonathan dropped like a slaughtered cow.

The impact jarred Kenny's wrist. Carried by his own momentum, he stumbled over Jonathan and fell.

As Jonathan tried to climb to his knees, Kenny scrabbled round for the crowbar, found it, took it in two hands, got to his feet and hit Jonathan with it.

Jonathan fell down again, tried to raise himself, crawl away.

Kenny stamped on his kidneys, kicked him in the guts, the ribs. He stamped and kicked until Jonathan stopped moving. Then, gulping for air, he said: 'Get in the van.'

'What are you doing?'

Kenny raised the crowbar, breathing through his teeth.

'Please,' said Jonathan.

Kenny kicked him in the head.

Jonathan raised a hand in submission and, mumbling *please*, dragged himself towards the Combi — Kenny prodding and goading him with the crowbar.

When Jonathan had reached the Combi, Kenny shoved him into the front passenger footwell. 'Curl up and shut up.'

He lay down where Kenny told him. Kenny had to push the passenger seat back to its fullest extent. Then Kenny got behind the wheel, tossed a blanket over Jonathan and drove away, the crowbar on the seat next to him.

He drove under the limit until he reached the darkness on the edge of town, parking in a gravel lay-by on the perimeter of a cow field. The Combi was sheltered by an immense overhanging oak.

Kenny darted round to the front passenger seat and dragged Jonathan out by the hair, making him walk with comically bent knees, like a trained chimpanzee. He opened the Combi's sliding side door and shoved Jonathan inside.

He wrapped duct tape round Jonathan's ankles, then his wrists, then his mouth.

This was done in night-silence, with heavy, laboured breathing. The unspooling of the duct tape was cinematically loud.

Then, hurrying, Kenny lay Jonathan on the floor of the rear compartment and threw the blanket over him again.

He drove Jonathan to the cottage.

21

Kenny drove down the dark, rutted lane and parked outside the cottage. He wrenched the hand-brake; a lonely sound out here, late at night.

Kenny looked at the black windows of his home. The Combi's engine ticked and cooled.

He stepped out and walked for a bit in the darkness, stretching his legs.

There was a silky rustle in one of the hazel trees bordering the driveway. Perhaps it was one of the saucer-eyed owls that nested here.

Kenny knew that, if he stood still for long enough, the night would come alive all around him. In the darkness were bats and moths and badgers. There were worms and mice and rats and foxes. Moles burrowed beneath his feet.

He dug out his keys and let himself in. He'd been gone long enough, and far enough, that he could smell the cottage, slightly musty, like the bottom of an empty biscuit tin; the smell of home.

Without turning on the lights, he went to the kitchen. He took a serrated steak knife from the drawer, then took the blue plastic bucket from the cupboard under the sink and filled it with cold water.

He carried the bucket to the Combi, water sloshing his toes. He slid open the side door and tugged the blanket from the shape in there.

Beneath the blanket, Jonathan was conscious — wide-eyed as an owl. So Kenny didn't need the cold water to wake him, but he tossed it over Jonathan anyway.

Jonathan howled, stifled by the duct tape. He lay there, drenched and shivering as Kenny showed him the knife.

When it had registered in Jonathan's eyes, Kenny slit the tape that bound Jonathan's feet and said, 'Walk to the house.'

Jonathan struggled to a woozy sitting position. He perched on the edge of the rear compartment, shaking his wet head to clear it.

He glanced at Kenny. Then he ran away, weaving, poorly balanced because his hands were taped before him like a penitent's.

Kenny cursed and followed. In one hand, he held the steak knife. As he ran, its blade flashed alternately silver and black in the moonlight.

Jonathan was following the rutted drive, aiming for the road that led to the village. Kenny ran fast and came close; he could hear

Jonathan's exerted breathing.

Kenny kicked out like a soccer player and tripped him.

Jonathan slammed into the ground and lay belly-up, eyeing the knife in Kenny's hand. He was panting, prepared.

Kenny grabbed a fistful of Jonathan's hair and yanked him to his knees. He dragged him to the cottage and shoved him through the door.

Worn out, Kenny shut the door and sat with his back to it.

Jonathan lay in the hallway, breathing in a shallow whine, watching the knife that dangled from Kenny's hand.

His helplessness made Kenny detest him. He wanted to kick him and beat him and scream obscenities, for being so impotent.

Instead he sat with his back to the door, saying: 'There you are, Jonathan. There you are. There you are.'

Kenny let Jonathan wriggle along the floor a little then stood and followed, nudging him towards the last of the empty bedrooms.

It was a cold room. Kenny rarely went in there. The only window, fitted with a crooked, salmon pink Venetian blind, overlooked a grassy incline to higher ground. It made the room damp in winter. The cold radiator was a white, cast-iron beast, ten fins marked with ancient paint splatters.

Kenny ordered Jonathan to sit in the middle of the bare floor and looked round for a few moments. His first thought was to shut the decrepit blind but then he thought again and used the steak knife to slice away its cord.

He made a loop of this strong, narrow rope and slipped it around Jonathan's throat. Jonathan struggled, gently enough at first, then harder. He stopped when Kenny held the knife to his eye.

Kenny tightened the loop around Jonathan's neck, just enough. He tied the other end to the radiator.

This arrangement made Jonathan sit with spine erect and head held high, like a proud dog.

If he moved, he'd choke.

* * *

Kenny left Jonathan leashed in the empty bedroom and walked around the outside of the house, through the long grass, past the rusting Morris Minors to the ramshackle outbuildings.

In one of them was a pile of timber — bits of cast-off wood which Kenny had collected over the years. He carried an armful of damp

2×8s round to the last bedroom window. It took two trips.

When the wood was collected, he peeked through the window.

Soon, it would be sunrise. Right now, it was still dark — especially here, in the shadow of the house. Kenny could just make out Jonathan, his back straight, staring into the middle distance.

Kenny returned to the outbuildings to get a hammer and some nails, checking out the sky.

He jiggled the nails in the palm of his hand. He knew that loud hammering echoing through the Levels was unlikely to wake his neighbours, most of whom were farmers. If they thought about it at all, they'd probably assume someone was doing some necessary repair — mending a gate perhaps, or a collapsed section of fencing.

Probably.

He lay the nails and the hammer in the muddy scurf next to the stack of timber and went inside.

Kenny locked the door with a big, black key. His legs were shaking and weak.

He sank to the floor.

Something inside his head was growing. It grew until it had occluded his vision.

He seemed to be speeding through a tunnel.

He saw a sword.

He saw a sunrise. A skeletal king on the green swell of an English barrow, the dawn breeze whipping at the remains of his clothing.

He saw a flaming bone glow red, like iron in a forge.

He saw the black silhouette of an ash tree.

He saw the burning eye of God.

He woke twisted on the kitchen floor, soaked in tears and sweat, knowing that time was very short.

22

Ollie had phoned Jonathan about half a dozen times, but Jonathan wasn't answering — not his landline or his mobile. So Ollie popped round to wake him up: Jonathan's place was only five minutes away.

He found the front door open and a half-eaten microwave curry on the coffee table in the lounge. He called out Jonathan's name and explored the weirdly echoing house. He found a broken window in the living room.

Not knowing what else to do, he went outside and called Becks. But Becks didn't seem able to grasp what he was talking about.

He kept trying to explain it: 'I thought he must've overslept,' he said, 'or had one too many last night. So I popped round. The door was open.'

'What door?'

'The front door.'

'Then where the hell is he?'

'I assumed he must be with you.'

'Well, he's not with me. Does it sound like he's with me?'

It was like he was trying to explain

quantum mechanics.

Eventually, Becks screeched to the kerb in her red Suzuki Swift and came clattering up the front steps. Ollie sat there waiting for her.

He waited while Becks ran her hands through her hair, looked at the sky, chewed on her lower lip — either because she was going to cry, or because she was angry. Or both, whatever.

'Fuck,' she said, 'Fuck.'

* * *

Becks scrabbled round inside her handbag and brought out her phone. She called Jonathan's brother Tim, in Sheffield, but he had no idea where Jonathan might be. He offered to come down. Becks told him not to worry. Then she hung up and called Jonathan's parents.

Jonathan's dad came to the phone. By now, Becks was beginning to snivel. She wiped away the snot with the heel of her hand and put on her smiling voice and said, 'Dennis! It's Becks.'

'Hello, love. How are you?'

She stood there, Ollie watching her; both of them scared to go into the house. 'I'm all right, thanks, not too bad. Have you heard from Jonathan at all?'

'What, our Jonathan? Last Sunday, was it?' His voice grew fainter on the line. Becks imagined him turning from the handset as he called to his wife: 'Was it Sunday our Jonathan came round?' A moment later he came back, saying: 'It was last Sunday. Why, love? Is everything all right?'

'I don't know, to be honest. We don't know where he is.'

'What do you mean, you don't know where he is?'

'He didn't go to work today.'

'Why not? Is he all right?'

'We don't know. His front door's wide open. There's food on the table, half eaten. There's a broken window. But he's not home.'

'Where is he?'

'We don't know.'

Ollie muttered something about quantum mechanics, but Becks scowled and turned away to complete her phone call, patiently explaining the same things to Dennis over and over and over again.

* * *

Ollie and Becks waited in the kitchen. Dennis and Elaine, Jonathan's parents, were there within the hour.

They walked straight in — it had seemed wrong, bad luck to shut the door that Jonathan had left open, as if shutting it might hamper his return.

Ollie and Becks were drinking coffee. Becks, who'd given up smoking eight years ago, had been puffing on Ollie's roll-ups. The cigarettes and the coffee and the worry had given her a shitty headache. Then she'd taken too many Nurofen. They hadn't made the headache go away, just made her feel like puking.

Dennis shook Ollie's hand, gave Becks a little hug and a kiss on the cheek. Elaine stood in the corner, clutching her handbag.

Ollie and Becks showed Dennis the broken glass in the living room, the half-brick.

Dennis said, 'Did anyone call the police?'

Ollie and Becks, both in their mid-thirties, were relieved that a responsible adult had arrived to ask such questions. In unison, they said, 'Not yet.'

Dennis took out his mobile, dialled 999 and said: 'Police, please.'

Elaine began to cry.

Becks sat on the sofa, drained.

Ollie went out to the garden. He made himself a single-skinner, sucking it half to death on the patio, watching the wind play in the poplars at the foot of the garden, thinking how badly they needed a trim.

23

Kenny was woken by the phone. He stood, awkward and bewildered, wondering for a bleary moment where he was and why his arms and legs ached so much.

Then he remembered, and answered, 'Hello?'

Pat said, 'You're back then?'

'Mmmm. What time is it?'

'Gone nine. You up?'

'Yeah.'

'So put the kettle on, then.'

'Why?'

'Thought I'd pop over.'

'Why?'

'See how you are. How are you?'

'Good. Bit sleepy.' He thought of Jonathan Reese in the last bedroom and said: 'Look, there's no need to come all this way. I'll come to you.'

'I don't mind. It gets me out of the caravan.'

He couldn't think of a lie, so he told part of the truth. 'I've got nothing in — tea, coffee, milk, whatever. Let's meet in Weston. Have a stroll along the front.'

They arranged a time and place and Kenny hung up.

He stood, looking out of the kitchen window — at the ragged outbuildings, the barley fields beyond, the cattle, the fields of rape, the distant motorway. The vivid green hills, the bright blast of morning.

It was a clear day, but for a strange, hazy patch of cloud to the south-west. He walked round to the back of the house. He nailed the timber he'd collected earlier to the frame of the last bedroom window. He tested it for strength. It was good.

Jonathan Reese sat in the false twilight, cross-hatched by streaks of light which bored through cracks and fissures in the timber barricading the window to this lonely room.

Inside, Kenny told him: 'I've got to go out. When I come back, you're going to tell me what happened to her.'

Jonathan raised his eyebrows and made a noise, a single syllable. It was a question. *Who?*

'Callie Barton,' said Kenny. 'I want you to tell me what you did and why you did it. Because if you don't, I'm going to kill you.'

Then he left, locking the last bedroom door. He took a shower, got changed, and went to see Pat.

* * *

He was halfway to Weston when she called to say: 'Meet me on the front.'

'Why?'

'You'll see.'

He saw it long before they met. The strange haze he'd noticed was a black river of smoke surging up to the sky.

The Grand Pier was burning.

* * *

The pier was a sinister place, but it was an innocent one, too — it was two things at once, like a beast from a fairy-tale. Kenny stood on the sea front, part of the crowd that had gathered to watch it burn.

Pat found him. She edged up to him and said nothing, just took his hand and squeezed it once.

Weston pier stood on the second highest tidal reach in the world, and the tide was out — so here, on the beach, there was no water to douse the flames. A police hovercraft, helpless, drifted over the brown sand like a ghost.

There was a low death groan, a crash and a discharge of red embers — vivid and capering, fairies against the smoke-black sky.

The boardwalk collapsed. Superstructure rained on the beach.

All these people were here, at the edge of the land. Kenny thought they were like refugees waiting to be saved: the burning pier, the glowing metal; it was all a signal to the pale blue land across the water.

Pat said, 'I used to come here before the Beatles.'

And Kenny had come here with his dad, often enough; before the Sex Pistols.

He'd loved its optimism and its vulgarity. A pier, by its nature, was touched: a place of jangling and jangled nerves, shrieking and not sane. Kenny had felt at home there; riding the little train, losing his precarious balance on the seesawing floor of the Crazy House.

And now, as he stood witness to its ending, he knew that something inside him had changed.

They stayed without speaking for a long time. Later, when the fire had been contained, they wandered to a sea-front amusement arcade. It was weirdly deserted. They got change and stood next to each other, pumping coins into one-armed bandits.

Pat had to shout over the chinking and honking and flashing of the abandoned machines. 'Finished with your travels, are you?'

He shouted back: 'I think so, yeah.'

'No intention of running off again?'

'Probably not.'

'Because we were worried. Me and Mary.'

'You don't even like Mary.'

'I like her fine. It's Mary that's not too keen on me, but that's a different story. She's very protective of you.'

'I just had to go away and think.'

'About what?'

He shrugged. 'Y'know.'

'Are you going to tell her?'

'I'm going to try.'

'Because she's more important than the rest of it — lost loves, kidnapped boys. All of it.'

He nodded and said nothing because Pat wouldn't understand.

Outside, the summer sky was hazy with smoke, and the tide was coming in — brown, opaque, gritty water, not even really the sea.

* * *

After saying goodbye to Pat, Kenny stopped off at a DIY shop before driving home, where he dumped his carrier bags in the kitchen.

He took the claw hammer from beside the

kettle and shoved it through the loop of his belt then went to unlock the last bedroom, stepping from bright sunshine into fetid twilight.

The cord was still round Jonathan's throat. He'd fretted and fussed and stretched his duct-tape manacles, but they'd held.

Kenny scrutinized Jonathan with some satisfaction, like a nurse with a difficult patient. Then, using a sponge, he applied rubbing alcohol to the duct tape on Jonathan's face, massaging it into the bristly skin.

He picked at the corner of the tape. Soon, he'd made the corner edge large enough to get a good grip. He peeled the tape away in one long movement.

Embedded in the sticky side were flecks of Jonathan's skin and dots of stubble. His face was red as if sunburned.

He looked at Kenny and said nothing.

Then he exploded into something like a seizure. He bucked and thrashed in his bonds; he foamed at the mouth until the cord choked him and made him placid again.

Kenny had to fight not to giggle at the absurdity of it, standing in his spare room with a knot of cancer in his skull and a kidnapped man in the last bedroom, tied with nylon cord to a ten-fin, cast-iron radiator.

When Jonathan had stopped, Kenny said: 'Are you thirsty?'

'Yes.'

Kenny went to the kitchen and filled a mug with water. He carried the mug back to the last bedroom and knelt. He tilted the mug to Jonathan's lips.

'Where is she, Jonathan? What did you do?'

Jonathan gulped, water spilling down his chest. When the cup was empty, he said: 'I don't know where she is. And I don't know what happened to her. Hand to God.'

Kenny tested the weight of the claw hammer in his fist.

'I'm not lying,' said Jonathan. 'Please God. Please Jesus.'

They locked eyes. Kenny screamed at him. He screamed until his throat was sore and lifted the claw hammer, its buck-toothed metal end.

Jonathan said, 'Don't.'

Kenny lowered the hammer and squatted so he was eye to eye with Jonathan. 'If you tell me where she is, you can leave.'

The desire to believe this played on Jonathan's face like sunlight on a pond. Kenny watched it.

'On my mother's life. I don't know.'

'Then you'll die here.'

'No. They'll find me.'

'Who will?'
'The police.'
'They won't begin to look for at least a week. You haven't got a week. Because neither have I.'
Then Kenny saw an expression on Jonathan's face that he'd never witnessed before, not in person. He supposed it was terror.
He watched for several seconds, fascinated. Then he hurried to his studio to get a sketchpad and some charcoal, wanting to capture it.

24

In the morning, Kenny raised a bottle of water to Jonathan's lips and let him drink, warning him not to gulp — his stomach would cramp and he'd vomit. But Jonathan didn't listen and Kenny was forced to snatch the bottle away, as from a toddler.

Water ran down Jonathan's jaw and on to his chest. He sat gasping.

Kenny left him there, to grow hungrier still.

* * *

It was like having guests to visit. The routines of the day were disrupted and the atmosphere was different, but you had to get on and do things. So Kenny did the housework — dealing with the mud and the bloody footprints, all the rest of it. He pottered about, tidying.

Then he returned to the studio to add the finishing touches to his last portrait. Her name was Michelle. She was twenty-two and very pretty — a PA in a firm that made organic beers and cider.

Her married lover was chairman of the

company. He'd commissioned Kenny to paint Michelle after Goya's *The Nude Maja*.

Kenny had aged the painting — not well enough to satisfy the eye of an expert, because that would constitute deliberate fraud. The painting was aged just well enough that the client could hang it in his home study without arousing his wife's misgivings.

When the painting was finished, he'd build a pine crate in which to ship it. This was his favourite part of the job; wrapping the painting in newspaper and cardboard and bubble wrap, then wedging it tight into its flat pine crate and screwing the crate shut with a small Black & Decker.

He'd prop the crate against the wall, hand-addressed, to send by courier when all this was over.

Then he'd prepare some new canvases. He didn't know what for: they'd stay blank. But he liked preparing canvases almost as much as he liked dispatch; it required the expert repetition of long-learned techniques. It emptied his mind.

* * *

In the evening, Kenny visited Jonathan. He was carrying the blue bucket and the crowbar.

Leaving Jonathan tied by the throat to the

radiator, he snipped his hands free of the duct tape. Then he turned away, crowbar in hand, as Jonathan squatted to urinate and empty his bowels.

The air in the room grew rank and intimate. Kenny was reminded of a chimpanzee sanctuary he and his father had visited in Devon, back in the mid-1990s. Their concrete enclosures had smelled something like this. The desolation of that place — the sad-eyed chimps grooming each other — had sent Aled into a moonless depression from which he didn't emerge for many weeks.

When Jonathan was done, he stayed squatting there.

'Paper?'

Kenny threw him a roll of toilet paper which unspooled prettily as it flew, like a celebratory streamer.

Jonathan cleaned himself and pulled up the striped pyjama trousers Kenny had given him. Then he waited to be bound once again with duct tape.

When he was remanacled, Kenny put the bucket just outside the door and returned to Jonathan. He knelt before him and spoke the same words, chanting them in what had become a tender liturgy.

'Where is she?'

'I don't know.'

'Just tell me what you did. Help me. Then go home. Back to the world.'

'Oh, Christ. I don't know. I don't know what happened to her.'

'Just one question. Then you're free.'

'I don't know the answer!'

'*Yes you do!*' screamed Kenny. '*Yes you do!*'

There was a moment of stillness, paralysed and remorseful; then Kenny left Jonathan to another night of hunger and thirst.

He carried the bucket to the bathroom, emptied it down the lavatory, flushed, rinsed it with hot water, emptied it down the lavatory once again.

Then he washed his hands and left the bucket in the bathroom until tomorrow.

The phone rang. Kenny stopped to listen. It was Mary.

'You didn't come round. You haven't called. We're worried about you. Please call us back. Just pick up the phone and call us back.'

But he didn't. He couldn't, not until this was over.

He was sure it wouldn't take long — he'd already overheard Jonathan murmuring to himself, weeping, tormented by hunger and fear.

He wouldn't be able to stand it much longer.

Nobody could.

25

Becks was leaning across a desk at the police station, talking to a uniformed police officer. Jonathan's dad, Dennis, had come with her.

Becks said, 'The thing is, he's been really depressed. Really stressed out.'

The officer said, 'Stressed out by what?'

'The usual. Work. Money.'

The officer's name was Jenny Cates. She went through the procedure, taking details of friends and relatives, places that Jonathan was known to frequent; his medical history; his bank account, his credit and debit card details. She asked for a recent photograph, but didn't want to exacerbate an already delicate situation by requesting a DNA sample — toothbrush, a comb. This was for possible forensic comparison, should a body be found in a state of decomposition.

Now and again, filling out the form, she sneaked a glance at Dennis Reese. He seemed decent enough, hunched and defiant in his M&S windcheater, big-knuckled and full of shame.

As Jenny Cates wrote it all down, Becks said, 'What about the broken window?'

'The neighbours didn't report any disturbance.'

'Like they're going to. Who does that?'

Jenny Cates tried not to sigh before telling her: 'Most probably, he's gone walkabout.'

'His window was broken. Somebody broke his window.'

'Probably, that was just the straw that broke the camel's back.'

'He thought someone was in the attic.'

'In the attic?'

'Yes.'

'Who was in the attic?'

'He didn't know.'

'And *was* there someone in the attic, d'you think?'

Becks hesitated, embarrassed. 'I don't think so, no.'

Jenny Cates gave her a look, both sceptical and compassionate. 'Look, you'd be amazed if I told you how often something like this happens. He'll come back with his tail between his legs.'

'He runs a business.'

'People walk away from businesses all the time. Every day. Especially now — credit crunch, global downturn. Landscape gardening? Anything to do with the housing market, really — it's first to go. Best thing for you to do, try not to worry too much. Give him a few more days.'

'He could be in a ditch!'

'But most likely, he's gone off to think his problems through.'

'Christ, it's been days! When do you lot get off your fat arses and actually do something?'

Jenny Cates clicked her pen, to show that this meeting was over. She said, 'Jonathan will be listed as missing on the Police National Computer. An officer will be assigned and enquiries will be made.' She pocketed the pen. 'But chances are, he'll turn up. They usually do. Honestly. Meantime, try not to worry. If you need to speak again, you've got my number.'

* * *

Outside, Becks and Dennis waited on the corner until Ollie pulled up in the company van.

He leaned over to open the front passenger door. Dennis and Becks got in. The van smelled of vegetal matter and sweat and tobacco and sinsemilla.

Ollie drove them back to Jonathan's.

Dennis said, 'They've got it in for him. The police. Since day one, they've had it in for him.'

Becks and Ollie said nothing.

* * *

Dennis and Becks stood in the living room, looking at the boarded-up window.

Dennis said: 'You really think he did this? Our Jonathan? Threw a brick through his own window?'

'The police seem to think so.'

'Why would he do that?'

Becks shrugged.

Dennis pinched the bridge of his nose as if very tired. 'He hit her once, you know. The first one. That Caroline.'

Becks took a deep breath. 'Yeah. He told me. Truth be told, it sounds — not like she deserved it. Nobody deserves it. But she did provoke him.'

'Oh, she had a tongue on her, mind. She was vicious, that one.'

'He told me all about it. He's still ashamed of himself to this day.'

Dennis was looking at the floor now, whispering: 'I don't know where he gets it from. I never laid a finger on his mother. He never went without.'

'She made him unhappy, Dennis. Unhappy people do things they're ashamed of.'

'He never hit you, did he, love?'

'Not even close.'

'Good.' He nodded, still looking at the

floor, close to tears — not a man who liked to be seen crying.

Becks left the room, so both of them could go on pretending she hadn't noticed.

* * *

Elaine tidied the house and did the vacuuming and the laundry. She washed the bedding, so it would be nice and fresh for Jonathan when he got back. She scrubbed the toilet and mopped the hardwood floor. Then she cooked chops and oven chips and peas from the freezer.

After everyone had eaten (or tried to), Ollie tugged the strands of Golden Virginia from between his teeth and said: 'When he was burgled the other day . . . '

Everyone looked at him.

He hesitated and said: 'Well, what if it wasn't a burglar?'

Dennis scrutinized Ollie through his bifocals: 'Then who would it be?'

Becks gave Ollie a look.

Ollie shrugged. 'I don't know. I'm just saying.'

Elaine stared at Ollie for several long seconds. Then she stood, gathering up the plates, scraping the leftovers into the pedal bin. She began to wash up.

26

Late in the afternoon, Jonathan said: 'Can we talk?'

Kenny said, 'Of course.'

'I need food.'

'No.'

'It hurts.'

'I know.'

'I can't stand it. I'm starving.'

'It's only going to get worse. You'll get weaker.'

'This is torture.'

'Then make it stop. Tell me what I need to know.'

'I can't. I don't know.'

Kenny didn't get the chance to respond, because they were interrupted by the sound of a car pulling into the gravel drive.

Kenny hurried out to take a look and saw Mary's Fiat Punto with Mary behind the wheel.

He rushed back to the last bedroom, picked up the crowbar, jammed it under Jonathan's jaw. 'If you make a sound, a single sound, I'll come back here and smash your skull.'

Jonathan tried to nod, an indent in the flesh of his lower jaw pressed white by the teeth of the crowbar.

'Not a sound,' said Kenny, and left the last bedroom, fumbling with the big key in the old lock.

He was hiding the crowbar in the cupboard under the sink when the kitchen door opened and Mary walked in.

She looked elfin and beautiful, but she was scowling — and when she saw Kenny she started to cry.

Without saying anything, he embraced her. He was looking over her shoulder — down the corridor to the door of the last bedroom.

At first, she stiffened in his embrace. Then she relaxed: he could smell her moisturizer, her washing powder, her skin, even that she'd smoked a cigarette today. He could smell her tears.

She said, 'What is it? Don't say 'nothing'.'

Kenny was still looking down the corridor. Then he looked at Mary and held out his hand. 'Come with me.'

* * *

In a clearing on a low hillside not far away stood the relics of a stone circle, so little-known and forgotten that Kenny didn't even know if it had a name: eight stones, tapered at the top like flint axes, all but two of them long-since toppled and overgrown.

He and Mary had come up here many times. It was a good place, a restful place, charged with endurance and transformation — Kenny often thought of what had risen and fallen while these stones had lain here, in this earth.

They sat next to each other, their backs to the cold blue stone. The earth was baked dry beneath them and the sky was blue and they could see sheep and cattle, the distant motorway, the faraway village — and Kenny's cottage, white in its halo of green, the brook behind it, the sweep of driveway leading to its door.

He kept an eye on it.

Holding Mary's hand, he said: 'I'm dying.'

She turned to face him. 'What do you mean?'

He said it again. He told her about the aggressive tumour burrowing into his temporal lobe, his dwindling days on earth; the process of letting go the world like the string of a balloon.

She snarled and punched him in the upper arm, then clambered to her feet and called him names. He was a bastard, he was a selfish tosser, he was an arsehole, he was a spiteful prick.

Then she sat, not touching him or looking at him, looking at her own feet as he explained it again, more slowly, and she looked, watching the edge of the clouds, the world turning.

She said, 'How long?'

'Not long. A few weeks.'

'And there's nothing they can do . . . ?'

'Not really. Well, nothing you'd want to go through.'

She was toying with a blade of grass, concentrating on it. 'Come and live with us.'

'I'm sure Stever and the kids would love that.'

She laughed and punched his arm again, more gently this time. 'Then I'll come to live with you.'

'Mary . . . '

'Let me.'

'No.'

'Why not?'

'You've got the kids. And Stever.'

'And you're all alone.'

He wasn't. But he said, 'Can you imagine it? Me and you, living together — in a situation like this? It wouldn't be good. For me or you. It wouldn't be good.'

'Have you thought about — y'know. Places.

There are places. For when things get too difficult. Hospices.'

'It's on my list.'

'Can I help you find one?'

'If you like. It might be a bit depressing.'

'I want to help. I want to do something.'

'Okay. Then help me find a place. That'll be good. Find me a place. In Wales.'

'Why Wales?'

'It's where I should be. You know. Welsh blood.'

She looked at him, squinting. 'Okay.'

'Okay.'

She touched him, very gingerly. Stroked his forehead. 'Does it hurt?'

'Not really. Sometimes.'

'Where is it?'

He took her hand and guided it to the side of his head, just above his ear. The tumour squatted half an inch below their fingertips.

She withdrew her hand and rubbed it, as if it had been burned. She didn't know she was doing it. 'Can you feel it?'

'I get headaches, sometimes. I've been having seizures. I can see better, I can hear better. I can remember things as if it was yesterday, just like old people say. But it's true. As if it was this morning. You remember all the camping trips? In the Combi, to the beach?'

She could remember them all, but she couldn't bear to talk about it. She said, 'What'll happen?'

'Maybe the headaches will get worse. Maybe I'll have more seizures, more often. Or maybe the headaches will get better and the seizures will go away. Nobody really seems to know.'

'It's not fair.'

'Oh, I don't know. In some ways, it's a good thing. You get to see everything. You get to see what's important.'

'And what's important?'

He didn't answer. She was silent and Kenny could see she was making the face she made when she was trying hard not to cry.

He thought about the day he'd left her, to come and live alone in this isolated place.

He'd embraced her and they'd wept: for each other, for all the things they'd felt and said, for the times they'd made each other laugh, nursed each other's fever, comically fallen over, burned food, made love. And they'd wept for their lost baby, a stillborn girl whom they'd never named and were never able to discuss.

They'd broken apart while promising to stay friends for ever. And as Kenny had moved his stuff into the hired van there had been an ache deep in his core, his spinal column, his organs.

He moved out to the cottage and became what he'd promised himself he'd become one day, a portrait painter.

Now they sat here, among fallen stones that had been just the same before they were born.

Mary said: 'Are you scared?'

'Not really. There's supposed to be this process: anger, depression, making bargains with God. After that, if I'm lucky, if I've got the time, I get to acceptance. But what's the point of all that, really? Who's got time?'

'Are you just trying to make me feel better?'

'Pretty much.'

Mary had nothing to wipe her face. Kenny took off his T-shirt and bundled it up like a rag. He gave it to her. She wiped the tears and snot from her face on the hem.

Kenny said, 'Stever's a good bloke.'

'I know.'

'And he's a great dad. He should get his hair cut, though.'

Mary laughed through her tears. She threw the bundled-up T-shirt at him.

He caught it and put it on. The hem was damp with tears and snot, but he didn't mind. What was the point of minding?

* * *

They strolled back to her rusty little Punto, holding hands like teenagers.

At the car, she leaned against the door and reached out to tug gently at the hair on the nape of his neck. 'How am I supposed to leave you?'

He didn't speak. She waited, then gave up, holding up one hand in resignation. She dug out her car keys and mimed 'call me'.

Kenny nodded. He waited until the Punto pulled away and was out of sight. Then he turned and raced back to the cottage.

He ran through the kitchen, banging his hip on a half-open cutlery drawer. He cursed and slammed it shut, then ran down the hall to the last bedroom.

He unlocked the door with fumbling hand, opened it, stepped inside.

Jonathan Reese had escaped.

27

Jonathan had wrenched the radiator from the wall; it lay like an art installation in the middle of the empty room. There were dark blotches on the floor where rank old water had leaked from inside the copper pipes.

Kenny took a moment to work it out. Then, abruptly, he grasped the significance of the open cutlery drawer — the one on which he'd banged his hip.

He rushed back to the kitchen but couldn't identify what might be missing; the drawers were always a mess.

Jonathan wouldn't know where he was, but he must have known a car was parked outside the front door. He must have known that Kenny and the driver of the car would be returning, although he couldn't know exactly when.

If Kenny had been Jonathan, he'd have run away from the car. That meant past the outbuildings and beyond.

Kenny glanced at his watch. He had no idea how long Jonathan had been gone. A fit man could probably have reached town by now, but Jonathan was weak and hurt and barefoot.

Kenny grabbed the crowbar from under the sink and bolted out of the back door, past the outbuildings into the dappled shadow of the great old trees. Junk lay scattered all over the oil-soaked ground — the corpses of Morris Minors. Bits of bumper, engine blocks, oily carburettors, torn seats, springs.

Kenny negotiated these with ease and pushed through the undergrowth at the bottom of his land. He ran past the old rope swing with the crumbling tyre. He knew the gaps, he knew where the brook could safely be crossed. Jonathan knew none of these things.

Kenny elbowed through the trees. They scraped at his face.

He found the stepping stones and ran across them, slipped, got soaked to the thighs, then scrambled up the opposite bank — snatching at exposed roots, hanks of grass, cow parsley. The soil was crumbly and inky black; it smeared his knees, got in his hair.

At the top of the bank, he moved along the hedge until he found the badger-path which ran underneath. He crawled on his belly like a slow-worm, wriggling his hips against rocks and soil until he was through the hedge. Then he stood with crowbar in hand at the edge of a sunlit barley field.

There was Jonathan at the other corner of

the field, running parallel to the hedge, towards the main road.

Kenny sprinted after him.

Jonathan turned and saw Kenny.

As Kenny caught up with him, he saw the knife in Jonathan's hand, stolen from his own cutlery drawer.

It was part of a set that had come as a wedding gift. Now it glimmered at him with turncoat malice.

Jonathan said, 'Just back off, mate.'

Their eyes locked and there was a moment of strange embarrassment — the tidal pull of normality. It seemed like they might suddenly laugh and walk away like men who'd jostled each other's shoulder in a pub. Then the moment passed and Jonathan was charging at Kenny, screaming.

He tried to stab Kenny in the guts but slashed him under the ribs instead, dropped the knife and ran.

Kenny had a feeling that was like a loud noise. He stumbled and fell over. He lay in the barley field clutching his side. He saw blood between his fingers, bright cherry red in the sunlight.

He fumbled with his other hand, looking for the crowbar. It was lost in the barley; then it was there, cold and slippy in his hand.

He lifted his shirt and saw the wound. There was something yellowish inside its lurid mouth: fatty tissue. But it wouldn't kill him. He stood up on Bambi legs and saw Jonathan throwing himself at the wild hedge, scrambling over it.

Kenny followed, hobbling. He limped to the hedge, struggled over the wide, spiky crest of it.

On the other side, among the pale haphazard trees, his feet slid in the rich soil and he lurched, wheeling his arms. He slid down the brook-bank, grabbing at loops of exposed root to slow his descent.

Jonathan was knee-deep in the brook, casting round. He found a branch — three feet long, wide as his wrist, lichen spotted.

Kenny could see it was windfall, weak with rot.

They faced each other: Jonathan in the water, Kenny on the bank.

Then Kenny stepped forward, sweeping the crowbar in a wide backhand that connected with Jonathan's skull and spun him backwards into the water.

Kenny dropped the crowbar, waded gasping into the cold brook. He straddled Jonathan, forced his face into the water.

Jonathan struggled, reached out, kicked. But there was no strength in him. Blood flowed from his ear, swirled, went pink in the water.

Looking across to the opposite bank, Kenny saw a kingfisher. He believed he caught its eye — a quizzical tilt of its head — before it flew away in a brisk, iridescent burst.

Kenny lifted Jonathan's head. 'Get up.'

On the third attempt, he managed it. Shambling, drenched, oozing with brook mud. Kenny thought how easy it would be to kill him — to cave in his skull with the crowbar and let him lie here, pecked by the birds, while Kenny trudged home to the cottage.

All Kenny wanted was to sleep.

Tomorrow, more rested, he could come back here and bury Jonathan by the brook's edge. The body wouldn't be discovered until Kenny was gone, and by then it wouldn't matter.

But he prodded Jonathan with the crowbar. 'Back to the house.'

Jonathan began to crawl like an arthritic beast.

* * *

Back in the cottage grounds, he made Jonathan stand at the furthest corner of one of the outbuildings. He knew the gravel, metal cuttings and bits of engine on the ground would cut Jonathan's bare feet, but they would stop him trying to escape, too.

Kenny shoved the crowbar through the loops of his belt, and rummaged among the junk that had been in the outbuilding for at least a decade — boxes, nails, plywood, carburettors and ancient, rusted-up tools.

The corners and the boxes were thick with cobwebs and damp. This was a private, mouldering place.

After several minutes' ferreting, Kenny found a coil of baling wire and lifted it, grinning in triumph. Dead beetles and roaches hung from it.

Kenny left the outbuilding, carrying the coil of baling wire in one hand. Then he beckoned Jonathan forward. Barefoot, Jonathan came mincing over the oily mud and sparse grass, like somebody stepping over hot coals. Each time he put down his left foot, he winced and took in a breath.

As they walked to the house there were a few moments where, theoretically, they might have been seen from the road — glimpsed through the hazel trees in a sequence of still images, as through a zoetrope. But Kenny needed to take this risk. He was weak and tired.

If Jonathan decided to run, Kenny didn't have the strength to chase him again. But Jonathan didn't run. He walked in a broken shuffle with head hung low.

They stepped into the house as if it had drawn them to it, to finish things.

28

In the bathroom, Kenny forced Jonathan at knifepoint to strip naked and stand under the cold shower.

Jonathan cringed when the water hit him. Kenny saw the violent gooseflesh, the pale, hungry body trying to raise its hackles. The water ran dirty, then clean.

Kenny sat on the lavatory. He was caked in brown earth, probing at the oval wound in his side: the crushed mouth of a goblet, the ruby red blood.

He was shivering with adrenaline. It made the pain seem far away.

He looked up to see Jonathan crouched in the enamel bath, naked and cold. They sat there for a while, both of them shuddering, before Jonathan said, 'This has gone too far.'

'I know.'

'Then just let me go. I won't say anything, not to anybody.'

'This isn't about me being arrested.'

'I need a doctor.'

'So do I.'

'Then call an ambulance. I'm hurt. Call a doctor.'

'Just tell me where she is. Tell me what happened to her, and all this will be over. Just say it. Just say the words.'

'I don't know what happened to her.'

'I know you're lying.'

'She left me. She went out one day and never came home. That's all I know.'

'That's not true.'

'I didn't hurt her.'

'You *hit* her.'

'Once. I hit her once. It wasn't right, and I'm not proud of it. But that's not the same as killing her.'

'You degraded her.'

'How?'

'By filming her. Privately.'

'People do that.'

'I don't.'

'No — you paint naked women for men to look at.'

'That's not the same thing.'

'It was a husband and wife having sex. She didn't object. She enjoyed it — being looked at.'

Kenny leaned over. Jonathan flinched. Kenny turned off the water and threw a towel to him. Jonathan draped it over his shoulders.

He huddled in the bath, shuddering. 'How do you know about the films?'

'I broke into your house,' Kenny said. 'I was in the attic.'

Jonathan said, 'Jesus Christ.'

Then he said it louder. He slammed his head against the white tiled wall. He said, *Oh Jesus Christ, oh Jesus Christ*.

Kenny sat on the lavatory and let Jonathan exhaust himself. He watched his blood, red mixed with brown, as it plipped and plopped on the tiled floor.

Outside, the sun shone bright in the evening. It had been such a long day; it seemed to have been going on for ever.

As Jonathan wailed the name of God and his own blood formed Rorschach pools on the floor, Kenny experienced a moment of panic — that this day was never going to end, that he and Jonathan were in hell already. And this was it, this little room. There was no escaping it. They were here for ever.

29

Mary got home to find Stever with Otis and Daisy in the front room eating omelettes and watching the end of *Hi-5*. Stever leapt up, kissed her on the cheek, bustled to the kitchen.

Mary said hello to the kids and sat Daisy on her lap.

Otis began to demonstrate the dance routine that went with 'Inside My Heart', but he wasn't able to clasp his hands to his heart and wiggle his hips without falling over. He landed flat on his arse, well padded by Buzz Lightyear nappies and jumbo cords. But he kept trying, and Mary and Daisy clapped along. When it was over, Otis shouted in triumph: 'Onetwothreefour — highfive!'

Mary held out a hand and Otis clapped it for her. Fat little palm, fat little fingers, smudged with ketchup and tiny flecks of broccoli.

Daisy said, 'Now can we watch *Hannah Montana*?'

'Really, sweetheart? I worry it's too old for you.'

'No, it's not! It's about two girls — they're

the same girl! One has yellow hair — the hair on the other girl is black — but it's the same girl! And her dad, in disguise he wears a fat moustache and speaks funny. Billyray!'

'Montana Montana!' said Otis.

Mary patted Daisy's arse; a signal that she was about to stand and leave the room.

From the doorway, Mary told them: 'Five minutes of *Montana Montana*. Then teeth, bath, book and bed. Otis, what are you reading?'

'*Bear Hunt*! Swish swish swish!'

'Daisy, what page are we up to?'

'The bit with the witch. I think it's like page five hundred or something. Or two hundred or something.'

'Right-o. You've got five minutes.'

Stever was in the kitchen, wearing a SpongeBob Squarepants T-shirt, cut-off Levis and flip-flops. He was making Steverburgers for himself and Mary, shaping the patties. Not looking up, he said, 'So how'd it go?'

Mary wanted to sit down, but there was nowhere to sit in the narrow kitchen. 'Oh, not so well.'

'Is he all right?'

She tried to say no, but couldn't speak. She began to cry.

There was a moment of panic as Stever

looked round the messy kitchen for somewhere to put down the uncooked, newly formed patty. Then he turned on the tap with his elbows and washed his hands, dried them on his cut-offs and hurried over to give her a cuddle. 'What is it?'

She was getting snot all over the shoulder of his T-shirt. She wiped at it, smeared it really. 'It's not good. He's not good.'

'I've said it before — living out there in the back of beyond, all by himself. It'll drive you mad. Why doesn't he get a place in town? All right, the market's not great, but — '

'He's dying.'

'He's what?'

She pointed to her temporal bone. Stever stood with his belly making a bulge in the SpongeBob T-shirt and his knees hairy in the cut-off Levis and his feet helpless in the flip-flops.

He said: 'Christ on a moped. How long?'

'Not very long.'

'Has he got someone to look after him?'

'No.'

'No nurses, whatever?'

'He wouldn't have them.'

'Jesus.'

Stever looked at the patties, arranged on the chopping board. Vegetable oil still sizzled in the pan. He said, 'He could move in here.

We could move the kids in together. Or move Otis in with us. If we shoved our bed against the wall, we could manage it. Otis wouldn't mind. And Kenny could have Otis's room. I mean, it's not much . . . '

Mary hugged him tight. 'I love you.'

'Don't be silly. Don't be silly. It's all right.'

When she'd disengaged, Stever turned to the patties. He lowered two of them into the scorching pan. 'Did you sleep with him?'

'I beg your pardon?'

'Did you sleep with him?'

Mary had a feeling like she was going up too quickly in a lift. 'Why would you say that?'

'He's alone, he's sick. You feel sorry for him. You want to comfort him. It would be understandable. It's all right. I just need to know if you did.'

'Jesus Christ, Stever,' she said, and stomped upstairs.

* * *

When she found him, later on, he was hugging Daisy the way he did when he was stressed or upset — as if she were a battery of infinite charge.

When he put her down, Mary saw him knuckle away a tear of excess love. This ursine man, with his long hair and his tangly beard, his cut-offs, his cartoon T-shirt, his flip-flops.

She felt helpless and sad. She wished, as she'd wished many thousands of times, that she could wiggle her nose like Samantha in *Bewitched* and make it all better.

But she couldn't. So she put the kettle on and made Stever some tea, proper tea in a proper teapot. And when it had brewed she poured him a cup and took it through on a tray with three Jaffa Cakes. This was code for 'I'm sorry'.

He accepted it with muted, embarrassed thanks. He took a sip of tea and said, 'Mmm, lovely', which was code for 'me too'.

Mary said, 'I promised to help him find a place. You know — one of those places where you go.'

'We can do that,' said Stever. 'That's something we can do.'

30

Kenny made Jonathan carry a kitchen chair to the last bedroom. They were both fatigued and injured and it wasn't easy. Jonathan stumbled, trying to manoeuvre the chair sideways through the narrow door.

Then he placed the chair in the middle of the room and sat on it. Kenny used the baling wire to secure his wrists and ankles.

Jonathan said, 'I've got no circulation. It's too tight.'

'You should have thought of that.'

'And my knee hurts. It's seizing up.'

'You should have thought of that, too.'

'I'm thirsty.'

'So tell me about Callie Barton, then drink all the water you want.'

'You do know the police are probably looking for me.'

'No, they're not.'

'But what if they are?'

Kenny limped away. He closed and locked the door and stood in the kitchen. There were smears of mud and blood on the tiles; dirty, disordered footprints.

He returned to the bathroom and stripped

and ran the water over himself. Then he turned off the shower and sat on the edge of the bath, probing the gash under his ribs.

It wasn't deep, but it was ugly, a pink and creamy mess, its lips already a rich necrotic purple.

He glugged half a bottle of TCP into it. When he'd stopped howling, he opened the first aid kit and pressed a couple of large plasters across it.

Then he strapped himself up with duct tape, wrapping it round and round and round his belly.

He took his medication from the bathroom cabinet. Before he could remove and swallow the first pill, his jaw went into spasm.

He fell.

His head hammered on the bathroom floor.

A shadow passed over him like a crow.

In its wake, he lay curled on the floor. Night things were alive all around, cockroaches, rats, mice. But he saw nothing, because the ugly strip-light glowed overhead, blinding him.

He thought *please, please* and at the end of it the sunrise came, lending him another day.

He crawled to his knees then his feet, knowing the next seizure would kill him.

31

Kenny walked out to the crow-call of early morning, limping a bit, the horrors of the long, paralysed night grinning at his shoulder. He drove a few miles to the garden centre at the edge of town.

When he got back to the white cottage in its little spray of morning light, he dumped the plastic bags on the threshold of the last bedroom.

Jonathan was dozing in the semi-darkness, his head lolling on his chest like Kenny's sometimes did on aeroplanes.

He woke when Kenny knelt to snip away the wire manacles. He replaced them with plastic cable ties, the kind used to bundle up electrical cords or secure hubcaps to wheel rims. Kenny fixed them tight to Jonathan's wrists and ankles, then joined each to the frame of the chair with a second cable tie.

As he worked, he said, 'These won't cut off your circulation — not unless you pull on them. You're not strong enough to snap the plastic. All that'll happen, they'll tighten and start to hurt.'

Then he closed the bedroom door, locked

it with the big black key, and phoned Pat.

She said, 'How are you, cocker?'

'I'm good.'

'Did you speak to Mary?'

'Yes.'

'Good for you. How'd she take it?'

'Pretty well, I suppose. She cried a bit.'

'That's good.'

'Is it?'

'It means she's not in whatsit, denial. If she's had a few tears already, it means she knows it's really happening. You fancy some company?'

'Not today. I've got stuff to tidy up. Things to do. Loose ends and whatnot. I'll give you a call later on. Tomorrow, maybe?'

'All right then, china. Look after yourself. Call if you need to.'

'Will do.'

'Seriously,' she said, 'look after yourself. Thanks for calling. I appreciate it.'

'Bye, Pat.'

'Bye, love.'

She hung up.

* * *

Pat hung up, and stood in the kitchenette with the phone in her hand as if she'd forgotten something. Then she went to her handbag and dug out her little notebook. She called Mary at work to ask how she was.

Mary said: 'How long have you known?'

'Not long.'

'So why not tell me?'

'He made me promise, love.'

'Right. Of course. I'm sorry.'

'Don't be. So how are you?'

'To be honest, it's knocked me for six, like I'm in shock or something. I don't know what to do with myself.'

'It'll do that.'

'And what about you? It must have been terrible, being the only one who knew . . . '

'Tell the truth, I didn't know what to think. He seemed to be wearing it so lightly.'

'That's Kenny. He puts on a face for the world.'

'So how do you think he is?' said Pat. 'I mean, really. In himself. How do you think he's coping?'

'Why? Is something wrong?'

'No. Nothing's wrong. It's just — I've just got off the phone with him. He sounds tired, much more tired than the last time we spoke. I just wanted to know what you thought.'

'You know the weird thing? The weird thing is, we spent some time together. We went for a walk, we held hands — up there by the standing stones. We talked and talked, but

I can hardly remember any of it.'

'That's not weird at all, chicken. It happens. It's just the way we're made.'

'Really?'

'Really. Listen, you stay in touch now.'

'You too. Thanks for calling. Do you need anything?'

'Oh, the fountain of youth, a young Adam Faith. Kiss those kids of yours. How old are they now?'

'Five and three.'

'That's a good age. You love them. Give them lots of love. You can't have too much love. That's the thing.'

'It is,' said Mary.

There was a silence, neither of them knowing what to say, before Mary hung up.

Pat shuffled to the banquette in her house slippers. Through the end of one of them protruded a big toe with a horny yellow nail.

She opened a book of Fiendish Sudoku and licked the end of a biro — one of those redundant habits there seemed little point in bothering to cast off.

Pat had been a copper for twenty-five years. You developed a gift for these things. She could try to ignore it, but she knew something was wrong.

32

Becks, Ollie, Dennis and Elaine had all moved into Jonathan's empty house, sleeping in the spare rooms and on the sofas. They'd become a strange simulacrum of a family. They waited, went quietly mad.

In the mornings, having decided the best thing he could do was keep Jonathan's business afloat, Ollie went off to work.

Dennis and Elaine hung around the house. Elaine did and redid the housework. Dennis did God knew what, except read the paper on the toilet for what seemed hours at a time.

Becks went to work and stared at her monitor and tried to find cheap flights for customers who didn't understand that she didn't set the tariffs and had no power to change them.

On Friday morning she woke up, had a shower and made up her mind. She went downstairs in her dressing gown with her wet hair combed back and told Dennis: 'I'm going to the newspaper.'

Dennis hated the newspapers; he hated what they'd done to his son four years ago and hated what they'd done, by extension, to him.

Dennis couldn't show his face at the golf club any more, and was ashamed by how much that bothered him.

Becks could almost hear him saying it: 'Let's not go dragging all that up again.'

But he surprised her. He said: 'You go to the papers, love. Make them coppers look like the shitters they are.'

* * *

Later that afternoon, Becks met Chris Bollinger in the park.

He didn't look or act like her idea of a journalist: he was a large, diffident young man in jeans and T-shirt, soft-spoken. He bowed his head as she told him everything — quietly at first, then quicker and quicker and with growing zeal until her nails dug into her palms and her voice grew strangled with outrage.

Chris Bollinger made occasional compassionate noises. He interrupted only now and again, to check a quote or seek clarification on a point of fact. But mostly, he just let her talk.

33

Feeling that time was growing very short, Kenny went to the drawer which contained Aled's portraits of him.

He owned fewer than ten photographs of himself as a child — some baby photos, a couple of faded, scallop-edged colour snapshots of a grinning toddler in socks and sandals. All had been taken by his mother.

But his father had left him dozens of portraits: on canvas, on paper, on napkins, in the margin of pages torn from foxed, Morocco-bound copies of *La Morte d'Arthur*.

Aled's sketches were frantic with love and the terror of loss, as if he feared the passage of each radiant moment. He sketched Kenny while he ate, painted him while he slept, drew his profile while he read the *Dandy* or watched *Buck Rogers in the 25th Century*.

When Kenny was gone, these pictures would become no more than items of passing curiosity. A stranger in a junk shop might flick through them and idly wonder what had became of this unknown, beloved child.

Perhaps Kenny was wrong about Callie Barton. Perhaps love just faded from the world like baked-in heat from a stone.

He couldn't look at the pictures any more. He packed them into a cardboard box and sealed it with Sellotape.

There were no paintings of Aled to pack away.

Kenny had painted him — his mad father, babbling like there were cities inside him, great metropolises, libraries, hospitals, barracks, vast cathedrals.

When Aled grew depressed, the talking stopped and he became sullen, heavy-limbed, beetle-browed. He'd painted Aled like this, too — but not until much later, when Kenny was nearly a man and becoming confident in his technical skills.

The first of these paintings, in burnt umber and swirls of inky black, Kenny called 'Still, Life'. Aled had wept when he saw it — his blue-black eyes with coal-red centres, his swirling orange hair, his grey beard.

That night, for the first time in many years, Kenny dreamed of Aled's wild, bearded face with its burning eyes and its great blade of nose.

And he dreamed of that lost painting — taken to the woods the day of Aled's funeral. Doused with petrol, burned, stamped on, wept over. Left to the earth.

* * *

Kenny woke twitchy, anxious and nauseated, a dry metallic taste at the back of his throat. The fragile scent of distant burning tyres.

Outside, the birds sang.

He took the list from the back pocket of his jeans and read it over. It seemed to belong to another time, like an artefact in a folk museum:

Mary
~~Mr Jeganathan~~
~~Thomas Kintry~~
Callie Barton

He could find no meaning in it; he'd forgotten Thomas Kintry and Mr Jeganathan. He'd forgotten Mary. There was only Jonathan Reese's defiance — and Callie Barton, whom he remembered with intense and growing clarity, as if he were moving towards her in time, not further away.

He replaced the list in his pocket and dressed, his father's face hovering on the edge of his consciousness like an after-image of the sun.

In the last bedroom, Jonathan awaited the ritual of the morning — the gentle intonation of her name, the appeal for confession, the promise of deliverance.

It was still early. Outside, the air was crisp but in here it was twilight and suffocating, like a birdcage under a cover.

Kenny was wearied of the ritual. 'I don't want to hurt you any more. Please don't make me. Let me put an end to this.'

'I already told you a thousand times. I can't tell you what I don't know.'

Kenny crouched down in the corner. 'How did you meet?'

'Me and Caroline?'

'Yes.'

'Does it really matter?'

'Yes.'

'Why?'

'Because if someone remembers something, it's not really over.'

Jonathan considered him for a long moment. 'We just met, like people do.'

'At a pub? A club?'

'At a dinner party.'

'Where?'

'In Bath. We were at one end of the table. We got on. She was funny.'

'Funny how?'

'I don't know. Just funny. She made me laugh.'

'What did she say, to make you laugh?'

'I don't know.'

'Well, what sort of thing did you talk about?'

'I can't remember.'

'Politics? Music? TV?'

'I can't remember.'

'How can you not remember?'

'We were flirting; it didn't matter what we talked about.'

'I remember every word she ever spoke to me.'

'When? Every word she spoke to you when?'

'It doesn't matter.'

Kenny thought of his class photograph: Callie Barton in the front row, bottom right. He said: 'What did it feel like?'

'What?'

'Killing her.'

'Oh,' said Jonathan. 'Right.'

Kenny didn't like his tone. He turned to stare.

Jonathan said, 'I used to get mail from people like you. Always asking the same question: what was it like? What exactly did I do, in what order? What did she look like, sound like, smell like? Was she naked? Did she piss herself? Did she gurgle? Did I fuck the body?'

'Shut up.'

'I thought you wanted to know everything.'

'Not that. Shut up.'
'Who are you?'
'Nobody.'
'What's your name?'
'Nothing.'
'Are you going to kill me?'
'Not if I don't have to.'
'But I can't say what you want to hear.'
'Then whatever happens is your fault. It's out of my hands. It's up to you.'

* * *

Struggling with anger and disgust, Kenny drove to the village shop to buy the things he needed: bread and semi-skimmed milk and microwave porridge. At the counter, he queued behind a young man in a suit who was buying cigarettes and breath mints.

Kenny handed his wire basket to the shop assistant, who passed the bread over the barcode scanner and bagged it in a Spar carrier.

Near the till were folded copies of the *Evening Post*. Kenny glanced at them. His heart stopped.

He reached out, picking up a newspaper and paying for it with change.

He walked to the Combi with the Spar carrier in one hand and the newspaper tucked under his arm. Behind the wheel, he unfolded the newspaper.

On the front page was a photograph of Jonathan Reese. He looked drawn, but younger.

The large headline read: 'MURDER QUIZ MAN DISAPPEARS'.

34

Paul Sugar plonked himself down into a creaking seat in the far corner of the empty café. He opened the morning edition of the *Bristol Evening Post*.

Above the fold, he saw the headline: 'MURDER QUIZ MAN DISAPPEARS' and scanned the story with practised disinterest:

MISSING WOMAN'S DEPRESSED HUSBAND VANISHES

POLICE DENY BEING SLOW TO SEARCH

The husband of missing Bath woman Caroline Reese — whose disappearance remains unsolved — has also vanished.

Jonathan Reese, a landscape gardener; has not been seen since 27 July when a family friend found the front door of his home open and his evening meal half-eaten.

Mr Reese was questioned at length by Avon and Somerset police after his wife disappeared from their family home in June 2004, but was later released without charge.

Mr Reese's current partner Rebecca Devlin, 33, a travel consultant from Yate, said Mr Reese has been depressed since his landscape gardening business ran into financial trouble late last year, and she fears for his safety.

Ms Devlin told the Post that 'the police don't seem to care' about searching for him, a charge Bath police deny.

A police spokeswoman said that Mr Reese's case had been treated in the same way as every other missing person case.

'We have not been slow to react. But we do need to wait a reasonable period before committing police time and resources to mounting a search,' she said.

Paul got the point, moved on.

His fleet blue eyes darted beneath the fold: 'Four Injured in Bedminster Bus Crash. Bristol Man's Extra Pint Leads to Court Fine.'

Over the page was a competition to win tickets to see *We Will Rock You*, which was coming to the Bristol Hippodrome. Then Paul got the feeling.

He couldn't describe it, other than to say it was a change in texture near the back of his head. It was the mild agitation he felt just before getting an idea.

He reread the rules of the *We Will Rock You* competition, wondering what he might have seen and not seen.

A picture of Ben Elton was saying: '*We Will Rock You* isn't just a title, it's a promise!'

Paul looked at that for a long time. Then he flicked to the front page and worked backwards.

'Four Injured in Bedminster Bus Crash. Bristol Man's Extra Pint Leads to Court Fine.'

'MURDER QUIZ MAN DISAPPEARS'.

Paul recalled sitting in this very café with Pat Maxwell, who'd begun to smell cabbagy and old. She'd been offering to pay him a pittance to find some woman.

And this man, this disappeared Murder Quiz Man, was the husband of the woman Pat Maxwell had asked him to find.

Paul stared at the story until his soy latte was cold.

He had a feeling.

Then he drank the latte with a scowl of disgust — waste not, want not. He folded the paper, popped it under his beefy arm, and went to work.

35

Kenny stood in the last bedroom with the newspaper in his hand.

'You're ill,' Jonathan said. 'You don't know it, but you are. You go into a trance. You've been stood there for ten minutes.'

Kenny looked down at the newspaper. He knew that Jonathan could see the headline: 'MURDER QUIZ MAN DISAPPEARS'.

Jonathan said, 'They're looking for me. I told you they would.'

'It doesn't matter.'

'Of course it matters. The best thing you can do now is let me go.'

'I'll let you go when you admit what you did. Just tell me where she is. Where did you bury her?'

But Jonathan brushed the question aside. 'Look, I don't know where I am. I don't even know your name. So you could drive me somewhere. Put me in the boot so I can't see anything, no landmarks or whatever. Drop me off somewhere. I'll give you fifteen minutes to get away, then go somewhere and call the police. I'll tell them I've lost my memory. They can't make me tell them where

I've been. Not if I say I can't remember. They can't make me.'

Kenny looked at him, tilting his head.

Jonathan began to shout. 'Come on! Jesus, this has gone much too far. And here's a way out of it! I'll never say a word. Not a word. I swear to God. Do you think I'm keen to talk about this, after what I've already been through?'

'What you've been through?'

'They ruined my life — the newspapers, the TV, the police. You've got no idea what these people do to you. And after that, the crank phone calls, the death-threats . . . '

Kenny waited until he was sure Jonathan was finished. Then he said: 'They're not going to find you.'

Jonathan nodded eagerly, as if agreeing. But he said: 'In ordinary circumstances, okay — maybe you'd have a point. But it's all over the newspapers now. They've *got* to look for me; it's a PR thing. Bad headlines. So they'll do a bit of house-to-house. Someone must've heard the window breaking, looked out, seen me chasing you. Maybe someone saw a camper van, a fight in the street. They might not have put two and two together yet. But a copper hears 'the night Jonathan disappeared, there was a fight in the street between two men, outside a VW Combi, not far from

Jonathan's house' — all they do, they go to CCTV. CCTV's everywhere. You can't move for it. How many Combis were in Bath that night? Half a dozen, tops? How many came within half a mile of my house? Not many. They'll have your number plate in half an hour.'

Kenny stood in the doorway, thinking about this.

Jonathan watched him. Then he said, 'They might have the number already. So the best thing you can do is let me go. Just let me go, and let this all be over.'

Kenny left the room, twisting the newspaper in his hand. He stood in the kitchen, looking through the window.

Then he put the twisted-up paper down on the work surface. Its edges darkened and softened as it soaked up some residual water.

Kenny went to his studio and found some writing paper and a biro. He supposed it would be possible for the police to get his fingerprints off the paper, but it didn't matter. His prints weren't on file, and time was short.

He walked to the last bedroom and dropped the notepad on to Jonathan's lap. Then he cut Jonathan's right hand free.

Jonathan said, 'What's this?'

Kenny stuck the scissors in his back

pocket. 'I need you to write a suicide note.'

'Not on your life.'

Kenny put the pen in Jonathan's lap. 'Just write the note.'

'No.'

'Write the note.'

'No.'

'Write the fucking note!'

'No.'

Kenny took the scissors from his back pocket and stabbed Jonathan in the arm with them.

Jonathan screamed.

Kenny yelled: '*Shut up.*'

But Jonathan kept screaming, bound to the kitchen chair by both feet and one wrist, bleeding from his upper arm.

Kenny held the scissors to Jonathan's eye and hissed through his teeth. 'Shut up.'

Jonathan shut up. He was breathing through his nose, sharp shallow breaths.

Then he began to struggle. Kenny moved the scissors so their point indented the delicate skin at the base of Jonathan's eye socket.

Kenny knelt, took a cable tie from his pocket and rebound Jonathan's wrist to the chair.

In the kitchen, he washed his bloody hands. When he was done he stood at the sink, letting them drip dry. He stood there until the pandemonium in the last bedroom grew louder, then louder still, and finally fell quiet.

* * *

Kenny took Jonathan's wallet and mobile phone from the kitchen drawer, put on some yellow kitchen gloves and cleaned them with kitchen surface wipes. He gathered up Jonathan's shoes, socks and shirt and put everything into a carrier bag.

He stuffed the carrier into his rucksack. It wasn't perfect, but it would do. Then he returned to the last bedroom.

Jonathan began to tremble.

Kenny strapped him to the chair with duct tape, reserving four inches for a gag. When Jonathan was mummified to the chair, Kenny slipped a white cotton pillowcase over his head.

Kenny watched him squirm like a worm on a pin, panting with fear and claustrophobia. He wished this wasn't happening. Then he looked at his watch. He had the sense that time had passed.

He closed and locked the last bedroom door.

* * *

Kenny stopped off in Bristol to withdraw two hundred pounds from an ATM. It put him into overdraft.

Then he visited a Carphone Warehouse, buying the cheapest pay-as-you-go mobile they had, cash. He knew the phone could be traced to this shop — and that he would appear on CCTV buying it. But it wouldn't matter.

In the glass arcade outside St Nicholas's Market he set up the phone, programming a single number into its memory.

Then he stuffed the packaging into the carrier bag it had come in, dumped the carrier bag in a bin on the way back to the Combi, and drove to Bath.

He felt that he was returning after a long absence. Smiling at the wheel in this fragile sunshine, he felt wistful for the person he'd been, the last time he was here — a man with no knife wound to his ribs, no hooded captive in his house.

He remembered parking the Combi at the campsite with the clean toilet block, having a lager and lime at the bench by the trout stream. In the sunset, the tourists had murmured and the midges had swirled like distant birds, and it seemed to Kenny that he'd been happy then.

But he hadn't been happy. He'd just had a

sense of purpose, which wasn't the same thing. Now that sense of purpose had become something else; he didn't know what to call it.

He drove in circles until he found a decent parking spot about half a mile west of Jonathan Reese's house.

Slinging the rucksack over his shoulder, he walked until he identified a path that would lead him once again to the Kennet and Avon Canal.

He tramped along the lonely towpath, watching iridescent dragon-flies hover-skip across the surface of the water.

Once, because his nerves were strained, he almost cried out in shock as a kingfisher swooped low and fast on the edge of his vision.

Just past the lock, the canal took a long curve. It was sheltered by an ancient hawthorn hedge. This was the right spot.

Kenny stopped and took several long breaths.

He waited.

Satisfied no one was coming, he slipped off the rucksack, moving quickly now. From the front pocket he removed the yellow kitchen gloves and put them on. Then he unzipped the main compartment.

From it, he removed Jonathan's shirt. It was filthy with blood and mud and God knew what else, but it would do. He folded the shirt like they did on display tables in shops. Then he lay it flat near the roots of the hawthorn.

He remembered the stories his father had told him — that hawthorn marked an entrance to the underworld. It was associated with the fairy-folk; not the glittering Tinker-bells of their century, but the dead, the demons, the demoted angels and lost gods of another. So it seemed fitting to lay these things here.

Kenny balled up the socks and stuffed them into Jonathan's Rockport shoes. He placed the shoes neatly on top of the shirt. Next to the shoes, he lay out Jonathan's wallet and mobile phone.

He walked along a few steps, then squatted to scoop up a handful of earth and dead leaves. He scattered it like ashes across the shirt, shoes, wallet and phone.

Then he reviewed this arrangement. These prosaic items, their presence amplified by strange context.

He thought of Oisin, kidnapped and trapped in the land of fairies. Then returning unharmed to learn that three centuries had passed. Crouching to touch the English soil. Becoming old in the blink of an eye.

* * *

Placed in the lee of the hedge, Jonathan's belongings might easily have been missed by casual trampers for many weeks. Kenny was satisfied.

He removed the yellow gloves and stuck them in his rucksack, zipped it up and headed back the way he'd come.

He walked for a mile.

Then, in weak sunlight — a few yards from a pathway that would lead him back into suburban Bath — he called the local police. This was the single number he'd programmed into the new phone's memory.

He gave them a false name and contact details. He said, 'I was taking the dog to do his business. He went sniffing in the bushes. He sniffed out something a bit odd. I thought you'd want to know about it.'

He described the shoes, the shirt, the phone. 'I peeked in the wallet, saw the name Jonathan Reese on a credit card, thought it rang a bell.'

He agreed to wait where he was, so he could point out the exact location of these objects to the police officers who even now were rushing in his direction.

Instead, he turned off the mobile and deleted the single speed-dial number from the SIM card. Then he removed the SIM card from the phone and, on the way back to the Combi, dropped it down a drain.

He polished the carcass of the phone on the hem of his T-shirt, inside and out, smearing beyond use any fingerprints he might have left. He dropped the phone in a bin at an unattended bus-stop.

Just before he reached the Combi a single police car passed him. He felt neither fear nor shame.

* * *

Back home, Kenny let himself in, running the kitchen tap until the water ran deep-underground cold. He slaked his summer thirst until his belly stretched, ripe as a berry, beneath his T-shirt.

Then he looked in on Jonathan, lifting the pillowcase from his head and peeling back the gag.

Jonathan's eyes were purple; his skin was damp and cheesy. He didn't seem to know that Kenny was in the room.

Kenny replaced the pillowcase over Jonathan's head. He locked the last bedroom door.

Later, when it was dark, he returned with the portable radio, to let Jonathan hear the news.

Bath police say they are 'very concerned' for the safety of missing Bath man Jonathan Reese, the search for whom took an apparently tragic turn today when items believed to be linked to him were found near the Kennet and Avon Canal. Sources close to the police say this might indicate a possible suicide . . .

Kenny waited until full awareness settled behind Jonathan's eyes, then turned off the radio.

Into the silence, he said: 'Nobody's looking for you. They're looking for your body in the Feeder canal and the River Avon. Your girlfriend and your parents are sitting down, right now, arranging a memorial service. Nobody knows you're here. You're all alone.'

He sat with his back to the wall. 'Just tell me what I need to know. Tell me what happened to Callie Barton. Just say it and go home.'

'There's nothing to tell.'

'I'm dying, Jonathan. I haven't got long left. If it happens, if I go first, you're going to die in that chair. You'll die of dehydration. That's quicker than starving. But first, it'll drive you mad.'

There was silence in the darkness, just

breathing. Kenny was glad he couldn't really see him, tied to a chair, weary and famished and hurt.

In the defeated silence, Jonathan said: 'Did you want to fuck her? Is that what this is about?'

'No.'

'Because I fucked her. I fucked her all the time. She couldn't say no. Not to me. I made her come like a train. I made her beg for it.'

'Shut up.'

'Why? You don't want to hear this? I thought you wanted to know all about her. All her secrets.'

'Not that.'

'It wasn't anything special about me. She loved sex. She couldn't get enough.'

'Shut up.'

'She'd fuck anything. Black, white, tall, short, fat, thin. She'd fuck strangers on trains. In pub toilets.'

'Shut up!'

'She'd fuck taxi drivers for the fare home. So are you the only man she ever met who didn't get to fuck her?'

Kenny punched him in the face.

Jonathan's nose bled in rivulets. Through it shone Jonathan's teeth. He was grinning, saying: 'That's it! That's it!'

Kenny punched him again. Jonathan was

still grinning. His eyes were jammed tight and he was sobbing, too. He was saying: 'Go on! Go on!'

Nursing his sore hand, Kenny stepped back. He placed the sole of his foot on Jonathan's sternum and kicked over the kitchen chair.

Jonathan's head struck the uncarpeted floor. It made a very loud, hollow noise.

Jonathan wasn't smiling now.

Kenny wanted to stamp down on his defiant face, to shatter Jonathan's leering jaw with the heel of his shoe.

But he knew it was what Jonathan wanted, too. He was scared of dying alone in this room, of going mad with thirst. He wanted Kenny to kill him.

Kenny took a breath, counted down from ten, counted down from ten again. Then he squatted and, keeping his back straight, hauled the kitchen chair upright.

The exertion tore open the wound to his side, the injury that didn't seem to heal.

Kenny looked at Jonathan and said, 'I'm going to have to start cutting off your fingers.'

36

Pat didn't read the newspapers because she found the stories just kept repeating: young men committed futile, degenerate crimes; their victims were other young men, children, the old. It just went wheeling on, careening down the hill, nobody able to catch it and stop it.

She didn't understand how this could be news to anyone.

She did watch the early evening news on TV, but mostly for the weather.

Tonight she was doing a Sudoku and only half-watching a police media briefing — flashing cameras, local journalists in dodgy suits.

The police chief sat there, facing the cameras. Behind him were posted enlarged snapshots of a moderately handsome young man whose age (late thirties, early forties) marked him out either as the killer of a close family member or the victim of some terrible, random crime.

The TV murmured on. Pat's eyes were on the screen but her attention was elsewhere — until someone said the name *Jonathan*

Reese and her mind snapped into place.

She brushed off a cat, leaned forward and turned up the volume.

The police chief was reminding the assembled news crews that, some days ago, a man called Jonathan Reese had disappeared. He'd walked out of his house one night and never come home. And now they'd found his shirt and wallet and shoes by the canal.

Pat knew that such irrational neatness was often taken to be a good indicator of a suicide's disordered frame of mind.

But Pat also knew who Jonathan Reese was. How could she forget?

Cutting away from the briefing, addressing the cameras from the streets of Bath, a perky television reporter disclosed that Mr Reese was rumoured to have been under considerable stress at the time of his disappearance. Apparently, the economic downturn had impacted his business, whatever that meant. So had the atrocious summer weather.

Back in the studio, the newsreader sat before a jagged graphic representing the fall in local house prices.

But Pat didn't hang around to see how much less her caravan was likely to be worth than this time last year. She was already looking for her car keys.

* * *

The door to Mary's house was opened by a hairy man in cut-off jeans and a *Battlestar Galactica* T-shirt.

Pat said, 'You must be Stever.'

'That's me,' said Stever and grinned through his beard, showing good white teeth.

Pat glowered at him. She couldn't help it.

Stever said, 'Come on in' and she followed him through to the living room, still bright in the evening sun despite the gathering cloud and the occasional shiver of rain.

Stever withdrew to what he called his Man's Room, pausing only to explain at tormenting length that he didn't mean the bathroom, he wasn't going for a wee or anything. Apparently the Man's Room was the little box room where he kept his DVD box-sets, his gaming computer, his DVDs and his comics.

He left, presumably too nervous to think about asking Pat if she'd like a glass of water. Pat was alone in the living room for a while, looking at her reflection in the blank TV screen.

Then Mary entered, barefoot in old jeans and a white vest top. When she bent to sit, Pat caught sight of a pale, freckled little breast, and felt a puzzling compassion.

Mary said, 'So what is it?'

Pat could see Mary's reflection in the TV screen. There they sat, the two of them.

Pat said, 'Did Kenny ever mention a girl to you?'

'I don't know. What girl? When?'

'Callie? Caroline, maybe.'

Mary gave the question a polite few seconds. 'No. Why?'

'Did he talk about the past? Before he met you?'

'Kenny? God, no. He always thought stuff like that was . . . ungallant. When we were together, he denied he ever looked at other women.'

'They all say that, love.'

'Don't they just. But the thing is — with Kenny, I believed him. We'd be at the beach. Or at the park in summer or something. And I'd make a game of it; I'd try to catch him out. All blokes ogle girls, don't they? Stever does it all the time. It's natural. Over the years, it's got so, I know his type — ' She mimed a pair of meaty breasts and a sulky, pouty mouth.

'You don't mind?'

'If they looked at him twice, he'd run a mile. He'd have to ask me what to do. It's sad really.'

Pat grinned at that.

Mary said, 'Why? Has Kenny fallen for someone?'

'I don't think it's that. But you know him better than me. Do you think he's — changed, at all?'

'Changed how?'

'Just changed.'

'Well, yeah. He's unhappy. He's wired — like he's on speed. He's got a look in his eye I've never seen before. Do you know what I mean? Like he's in the middle of something important.'

Pat knew the look: a secretive, raptorial glint.

Mary said, 'Has something happened I don't know about?'

'Is that the feeling you get?'

'Kind of, yeah.'

'Me, too.'

'So what is it? What's going on?'

Pat looked her in the eye. Mary had confirmed what she needed to know. But Pat had nothing to give her in return, no hard information. Just a feeling.

'I don't know, sweetheart.'

She took Mary's hand in hers and squeezed. 'The thing to do is love what you've got, not what you once had. Because one day the good stuff's all gone. And all you've got is the crumbs of the days that are left.' She squeezed once, for emphasis, then let go.

Then she heaved herself off the sofa, using her arms. She said goodbye to Mary and walked away from that Victorian terrace with a strangely determined gait, leading with her jaw, heading towards her little car.

* * *

Mary stood at the window, watching. She wondered where Pat was going and what she was going to do when she got there.

The first thing Mary did was go and see the kids. They were asleep. She was filled with a tenderness so acute it bordered on grief.

Then she went to the Man's Room. A yellow radiation warning sign was pinned to the door, and drawings by the kids — Wallace and Gromit, Happy Feet, a pony with a machine gun.

Stever was playing *World of Warcraft* on a gaming computer for which he'd paid what another man might have spent on a pretty decent second-hand car. Stever still owned the Jurassic Corolla that had been fifteen years old when Mary met him. All these years later, no power on earth could prevent it from smelling a bit like spoiled milk.

Mary sat in his lap and kissed him. She ran

her fingers through his coarse mane, in need of a comb; she nibbled his sweet little earlobes, she gave his balls a gentle squeeze.

He said, 'Is it Christmas?'

'Pat told me to do it.'

'Pat told you to come upstairs, interrupt my game and squeeze my nuts?'

'Pretty much.'

'I liked her,' Stever said, 'the minute I saw her. Have her round any time you want.'

Mary said, 'Perhaps it's time to turn the computer off.'

Stever put down the mouse.

37

Kenny was in the studio with his portraits of Jonathan — a series of impatient sketches, smudged with jaundiced ochre, charcoal, dabs of scarlet. Laid out in a sequence, they formed a map of his degradation from frightened human being to something leaner, injured, more brutish.

Jonathan would never be released from the last bedroom while these sketches existed. They gave Kenny power.

He was interrupted by the sound of a car in the drive. It wasn't Mary this time — he knew the sound of her engine like he knew the rhythm of her footsteps.

He ran to the window and saw Pat's Peugeot bumping along the rutted drive.

Kenny scooted back to the studio, vaulting furniture. He gathered the sketches of Jonathan and slipped them into a plastic portfolio, which he zipped and leaned against the studio wall. Then he ran to the last bedroom, where Jonathan sat strapped and bound to the kitchen chair.

His head hung lifeless and it seemed to Kenny that he might actually be dead. All he felt was relief.

But then Jonathan opened his eyes. His face was crusted with dried blood and a week's growth of beard.

At the sound of Pat's car door slamming in the driveway Jonathan grinned with white barbaric teeth and shrieked: 'Help!'

Kenny couldn't move.

He glanced over his shoulder.

The doorbell rang twice.

Jonathan shouted, 'I'm in here!'

Kenny closed the last bedroom door and picked up the roll of duct tape that still lay in the corner by the window. His fingers scrabbled to find an edge.

'Please!' Jonathan shouted, 'I'm in here!'

Kenny's fingernails found an edge. Fumbled. Lost it. Found it.

The doorbell rang again.

'My name is Jonathan Reese!'

Kenny's nails snagged the edge of the tape. He ripped off a long strip, raced over, grabbed Jonathan's face in a pincer grip.

'I am Jonathan Reese!'

He squeezed Jonathan's jaw until his lips pursed in a wet burlesque kiss.

Jonathan snarled, clamping down on Kenny's fingers with his teeth.

The bell rang again. Then Pat began to pound on the door; an impatient, copper's knock.

Kenny contorted himself, working hard not to shout in pain, twisting the hand, trying to free it. Jonathan bit down harder.

Kenny jabbed a finger into Jonathan's eye.

Jonathan opened his mouth to cry out, and Kenny snatched back his hand. He grabbed Jonathan under the jaw and applied the duct tape, not gently.

Jonathan tried to shout through the tape. He drummed his feet on the bare floor-boards. Kenny shoved him, hard: the chair toppled, fell over.

Jonathan lay dazed on his back. Kenny stamped on his belly.

Jonathan tried to take a breath. Couldn't. He lay there wheezing, blood bubbling at his lips.

Kenny hurried through to the hallway, locking the door. 'Coming!'

He grabbed a piece of kitchen towel, wrapped it round his bleeding hand, opened the front door.

* * *

Pat looked at Kenny, then nodded at his hand: 'What happened?'

He clasped the hand under his armpit. 'Caught it in the door.'

She walked in.

Kenny said, 'Go through to the studio. Make yourself at home. Let me clean this up.'

The studio was as far from the last bedroom as it was possible to get without leaving the cottage. As Pat waddled through, Kenny hurried to the bathroom, locked the door behind him and opened the medicine cabinet. He found a few plasters in a box.

He picked blood-sopping paper fragments from the bite wounds to the middle fingers of one hand; tattered half moons, oozing blood and plasma, clearly showing the impression of Jonathan Reese's teeth.

He ran cold water over the cuts then, using his teeth and one hurried hand, applied a plaster to each of the gashes.

As he did so, he caught sight of his reflection in the medicine cabinet and shut down for a moment, staring.

Usually, when Kenny looked in a mirror, he knew himself. But he no longer recognized this man. His hair was sticking up. He was unshaven and pale. His wrinkles had deepened. His eyes had gone wrong. It was as if someone else was looking out through them. He thought of a face burning in a forest.

He blinked, slow as a lizard basking on a rock, and looked away. He unlocked the bathroom door and walked out to join Pat in the studio.

* * *

Night rain was falling on the glass ceiling and Pat was looking at the painting of Michelle. Kenny stood at her shoulder.

She said, 'And who's this?'

'Client. You sound a bit tetchy.'

'By 'client' you mean your client's crumpet.'

'I suppose.'

'Why have you been avoiding me?'

'I haven't.'

'You want me to ask again? I'll stand here and I'll keep asking. I don't get bored.'

'I've been busy.'

'Doing what?'

'Stuff.'

'So much stuff you can't pick up the phone?'

He flexed his jaw, moved his tongue round his mouth, couldn't find any words.

She said, 'Are you eating?'

'Yes.'

'You look rough. What was all the shouting?'

'What shouting?'

'I heard shouting.'

'When?'

'When I rang the doorbell.'

'I hurt my finger. I might've shouted. Did I shout?'

'Someone did.'

'There you go then.'

'What's happening over there?' She nodded towards the last bedroom.

'Nothing. Why?'

'You keep looking.'

'Do I?'

'You got guests I don't know about? Having a Nazi-themed orgy?'

'Ha! No, no. I've got a rat though. I think it's a rat.'

'You should get a cat.'

'It hardly seems worth it, really.'

'So how did you kill him?'

There was a noise in Kenny's head like a train rushing past. He listened to it, blinking.

Pat said, 'I'm not so old I'm completely doolally. How did you do it?'

Part of him — the old part — wanted to tell her the truth, that Jonathan Reese was alive in the last bedroom.

But what good would that do? Pat would call the police. They'd cut Jonathan loose, give him food and water, set him free.

Nobody would ever know what happened to Callie Barton: and Pat would learn what kind of creature Kenny had become, in the name of pure love and dead days. So he said, 'Does it matter?'

She was looking past him now, at their reflection in the studio windows. She laughed. 'You selfish little fucker.'

'Pardon?'

'That girl Mary, she loves you. Stever loves you. Even their fucking *kids* love you. And all you can do is wrap yourself up in something that happened thirty years ago, that means fuck all to anybody.'

'It's not like that.'

'Then what's it like?'

For a moment, Kenny thought Pat was going to hit him. But she just said: 'Me — I can hardly remember being a kid. Not really. I look at a photo of this little girl I used to be. There's no connection.' She was still looking out of the window. 'Time passes. It just does.' Then she turned from the window and said: 'What if Jonathan Reese didn't do what you think he did?'

'He did.'

'But what if?'

He kept his silence.

Pat said: 'If Mary and Stever ever find out what you did, it will kill them.'

'Will they find out?'

'Don't put this on my shoulders. This isn't

my doing. Do you want to protect Mary from this?'

'Yes.'

'Good. Me, too. That's why I'm here. To protect her. Have you made a will?'

'Yes.'

'Who gets the house?'

'Mary. Are you going to tell her?'

'Are you listening to a single sodding word I'm saying? What kind of twisted bitch do you take me for? The reason I came here tonight, I didn't come here for you. I don't care about you, not any more. I care about Mary. Because she doesn't deserve all this. The weight of what you did. She doesn't deserve it.'

'I know.'

'She can never know.'

'So don't tell her.'

'I never would. But I'm not the only one you have to worry about.'

For a moment, Kenny thought he might faint. 'What?'

'There's someone else.'

'Who?'

'A man called Paul Sugar.'

'Who the hell's that?'

'The man I paid to find Callie Barton.'

'The man you what? Why?'

'I wanted to help, Kenny. But I'm tired.'

Kenny was shamed by his burst of anger, and too worn out to maintain it. He sagged and said: 'What does he know?'

'I can't say for sure — not yet. I do know he'll have read the papers and made the same connection I did.'

'Will he go to the police?'

'Have you ever met a really greedy man, Kenny?'

'Yes.'

'Well, double him and add one more for luck. That's Paul Sugar. Do you own this house outright?'

'No. But my life insurance will cover the rest of the mortgage.'

'And the house is worth a bit?'

'Not as much as it was last year. Where are you going with this?'

'You need to make out a new will. Leave everything to Paul Sugar.'

'I can't do that.'

'Yes, you can. Right now, Paul doesn't know the full story. Odds are, he won't even care about the full story. What he cares about is money. Promise him enough, he'll stop being interested.'

'The house goes to Mary.'

'The house is the price Mary has to pay for your secrets. You need to see your solicitor.'

'Jesus Christ.'

'Don't throw that name around too lightly. Not in your position.'

He saw that she was not joking. He said, 'And what about me and you?'

'What do you want me to say?'

'That you forgive me?'

'For making me an accessory to murder? I don't think so.'

'Will you?'

'If I forgave a bit better, I'd have retired Chief Inspector. And I wouldn't be living in a fucking caravan.'

'Please, Pat.'

But she just made a face, a disgusted face, and made for the door.

Before getting there, she turned. She said, 'You hung me out to dry, you self-centred little twat.'

* * *

Kenny waited for the sound of her engine, the wheels growing more distant on the gravel drive. He was trapped behind an alien face.

When Pat had gone, he went to the outbuildings. They were mostly in darkness, now the sun was setting.

He probed round with a wan torch until its beam alighted on an eight-gallon container, far in the dark corner. He brushed cobwebs from the container, smelled it, then hoisted it and returned to the house.

He grabbed a Bic lighter from the kitchen drawer and took a page from the free-sheet that lay unread on the kitchen table. He twisted it up, then stuffed it into his back pocket.

He went through to the last bedroom.

Jonathan was still lying flat on his back, tied to the chair.

Kenny unscrewed the lid of the container and splashed petrol over Jonathan's face, head and upper body.

Then he produced the Bic lighter. His hand was not shaking.

38

Jonathan roared, stifled by the duct tape. He shook his head as though denying a terrible accusation.

Kenny crouched down to rip the tape from Jonathan's mouth. Soaked in petrol, it came free easily.

'Okay,' said Kenny, 'you're not scared to die. But you don't want to burn. Nobody wants to burn. Do you?'

'No.'

'Did you hear the conversation I just had?'

'Some of it.'

'Then you know time's run out.'

'I can't tell you a story just to make you feel better.'

'Then I'm sorry. We're done.'

Kenny limped from the room.

In the doorway, he lit the end of the twist of newspaper.

Jonathan followed him with his eyes. He was breathing fast, like he'd been running.

Kenny stepped forward, ready to toss the taper into the room.

Jonathan shouted: 'All right.'

Kenny lowered the taper. 'What does that mean?'

'It means, all right. I'll tell you what you want to hear.'

'And what's that?'

'I'll tell you what happened. But put out that fire. Please put it out. Put it out and I'll tell you.'

Kenny took the taper to the kitchen, far from the petrol fumes, and ran it under the tap.

Then he returned to Jonathan and crouched down like an archaeologist, his elbows resting on his knees.

He was looking down into Jonathan's eyes.

He said, 'All right. Tell me.'

39

Kenny sat against the wall. Jonathan lay on his back, tied to the chair. It was as if the fabric of reality had been twisted between them.

Jonathan said, 'Are you sure?'

Kenny said, 'Yes.'

Jonathan shifted, as far as he was able. 'There's not much to it, really. I was ill. Depressed. About a year before, we'd had this really bad argument, the one where I hit her. She took me back, but she wasn't happy. Neither of us was happy. She wanted things to be different. She was bored with where we lived, bored with our friends, bored with her job. Bored with me.

'She'd started taking these night classes, talking about doing another degree, something to do with English. She wanted to change her life, become a teacher, whatever. I don't know; nor did she, really. She was having an affair with this bloke. Callum, his name was. He was, like, her first love — from school. They got talking on the internet. Met up somewhere, some bar in Bristol. Started sleeping together pretty much straight away, as far as I could work it out — probably in the back of his car, that night. That used to kill me, for some reason: thinking about them in the back of his shitty little car. That was worse than anything.'

'So you knew about it?'

'From the beginning, pretty much.'

'How?'

'You can just tell. I used to read her emails to him, their texts. All this sickly talk: 'I'd love you to be the last thing I see every night and the first thing I see every morning.''

He made a sour face, rehearsing his own disgust.

'Did you talk to her about it?'

'No. I thought it was one of those things she had to do, just her way of getting back at me. I'd decided to let it burn itself out. But the jealousy, mate. Jesus. It's like having a monster living inside you, like you become an ogre. I started drinking again, getting ugly drunk. Falling over drunk.'

His face was far away now. Kenny let him have the moment he needed.

'So one night, she comes home really late. Tarted up to the nines. She's a bit drunk. I'm drunk, too. I tell her she's making a fool of herself, mutton dressed as lamb, showing herself off like that.'

He glanced at Kenny, but Kenny was

staring at the wall as if at a screen. So Jonathan went on.

'So I'm shouting at her. She's fucking this, she's fucking that. And halfway through — I'm still shouting — she gets a text message. A little beep. She reads it. And she laughs. I think the text is from him, from Callum fucking Murray, Mr Fuck You Till You Scream in the Back of My Mondeo. She's so besotted with him, I'm so meaningless. I'm ranting and raving. And she's smiling at his text message. So I punch her.'

'And?'

'She fell down. I pinned her arms with my knees, pressed a cushion to her face. She's screaming into it, screaming and screaming, trying to claw me, but I've got her held down. She's thrashing her legs around; she pisses herself, all down her tights. And then she's dead. Just like that. I'm alive, with this cushion pressed over her face — I remember the day we bought it, we'd gone to John Lewis to buy a chef's knife, but we came out with these cushions instead. She loved them. And one of them turns out to be a murder weapon. You could see it in her face. It wasn't like dead people on TV. She was just dead. Her expression was weird. I can't describe it. Her eyes were all funny.'

'So what did you do?'

'Panicked. Put her in a composting bag and dragged her out to the van. Picked up her handbag, her mobile phone. The lot. Took her out near Bath Valley Woods. There's an old farm down there — derelict. I used to go birding there when I was a kid.'

'Birding?'

'Bird watching. I knew the land — I knew there was an old cesspit. Not used for years, covered up with corrugated iron. I drove as close to it as I could. Took her the rest of the way in the wheelbarrow. Still in the bag. Her foot was hanging out. I thought someone was going to see me. Then I got to the cesspit. Cut the lock, chucked her in.'

'You threw her in a cesspit?'

'It's not the kind of place where people look, is it? And any — y'know. Any weird smells, people aren't going to think too much about it. Worst comes to worst, they're going to think it's a dead fox. A dog, a badger. Whatever.'

'And that's it?'

'What did you want to hear?'

'I don't know.'

'No. Well — now you know.'

'I do. Yeah.'

'For weeks and weeks it was like I was outside my body. I wanted to kill myself. I couldn't think about anything else — just how to do it, when to do it. For months, this was. Years, really.'

'Why didn't you do it?'

'Thinking about my mum and dad, how they'd feel if I did it. And then, bit by bit, it all just started to fade away — the police, the newspapers, the death threats. It began to seem like it never happened. It still does, to be honest. It seems like none of it ever happened.'

Kenny sat there, staring at the wall. 'Things just pass,' he said.

Jonathan turned his head, facing him. 'So does it feel better? Knowing?'

Kenny didn't know. He didn't have a name for what he felt. He'd only felt it once before, when the doctor told him he was dying.

He stood up and said, 'I'll be back in a minute.'

He walked away, feeling Jonathan's eyes on his back.

* * *

When he came back, two hours later, he was carrying an old analogue tape recorder.

40

Pat left Kenny's cottage, drove two or three miles through country roads, then pulled over. She took in a big breath, held it for a moment, released it with a shudder.

For several minutes she had to fight the urge to vomit, breathing quickly and flexing her fists so hard her fingernails bit deep into the heart of her palms.

When it had passed, she dug out her cigarettes and cranked open the window, letting in the cool night and the rain.

She sparked up a John Player Special and smoked it to the filter. Now and again she was lit yellow by the sweeping eyes of a passing car. Once, she shone cold blue and ghostly in the xenon glare of a Mercedes.

She got out to stretch her legs. In the long wet grass at the edge of a cow pasture she dug out her mobile phone and called Paul Sugar.

'Pat!' he said. 'I had a feeling you might call. Where shall we meet?'

She felt a rush of affection for him, for his cheery dishonesty, for his self-knowledge and unabashed self-interest.

She said, 'My knees hurt too much to drive

all the way to Bristol.'

It was a lie, but she didn't feel too bad about it.

* * *

Next morning, they were strolling along the sea front in Weston-super-Mare.

It was public, but not as public as Pat would have liked. It had been a poor summer, and now the pier was gone, leaving just this blackened stump jutting out from the beach like a burned bone. There was hardly any reason for anyone to come here, especially this early on a weekday. The donkeys stood forlorn and unridden on the brown beach.

Paul was eating a hot dog. 'So what's all this in aid of?'

'I think you probably know.'

'Tell me anyway.'

Pat halted so abruptly that Paul nearly collided with her. He said: 'What?'

'You're not recording this conversation are you? No clever gear? No recording pens, whatever?'

'What good would that do me?'

But he lifted his big arms obligingly, thrust forth his dirigible belly, his prodigious hams, inviting her to pat him down.

Instead, she said: 'If you record this

conversation and try to use it against me — I swear on the name of the sweet Baby Jesus I'll come down on you like ten tons of fucking bricks. I'll come down on you so fucking hard and so fucking fast you'll leave a skid mark.'

'Jesus, Pat. Get a grip. I'm eating, here.'

'Good.'

They walked on. Paul said, 'So. You're in a shitty position.'

'You think?'

He had finished the hot dog and was dabbing ketchup from his pink lips. 'You come to me on behalf of someone you won't name, looking for this girl. Callie Barton. Turns out, she hasn't gone by that name since she was practically a baby. So I'm thinking, your client — who can he be? An old love? It can't be that — because the last he knows about her she was eleven, for Christ's sake. A pervert teacher? A paedo uncle? But I can't see you going for that. I remember how you had that nonce Harris by the balls once. You twisted his knob like a bit of liquorice.'

'I remember that. I nearly broke off his winkie-woo.'

Paul barked at that, appreciating it. And Pat grinned as she lit a cigarette.

Paul said: 'So anyway. You pay me to find out where she is, because you can't be arsed.

About five minutes after that, the husband disappears.'

'That was suicide, from what I read in the papers.'

He barked again, affably enough.

'The folded clothes,' said Pat. 'The watch. The phone.'

'Oh, come on.'

'You're a dick, Paul,' she said, 'but you're not a grass.'

'No. What I am, is in debt. At the very least, you know who did this. Which means, you're withholding evidence of a serious crime.'

'I'm a sweet little old lady. Who'd put me in the dock?'

'The CPS goes out of its way to prove how clean it is. It takes a look at you: ex-copper, into something a bit mucky. It comes at you with the full majesty of the law.'

'I'd do a month, tops.'

'You reckon? Well, that's your call. All I have to do is pick up the phone. We'll see.'

Pat said: 'There's a cottage.'

'What do you mean, there's a cottage?'

'It's not your personal cup of tea, I expect. But it's worth, say, two hundred thousand. It's yours, if . . . ' She mimed a zip over her mouth. 'You keep it shut.'

Paul grinned.

Pat bristled. 'This isn't a wad of greasy tenners in a jiffy bag, Paul. I'm buying you off. Good and proper.'

'So what's the catch?'

'The catch is, you'll have to wait.'

'How long?'

'Not long. I can't say for sure.'

'Not good enough.'

'Tough. Then make the call. Send me down. Stay in debt.'

'I need proof.'

'You can't have proof. What you can have is my promise.'

'What am I, off the banana boat? Have a house, Paul! Have this wonderful, invisible cottage. Fuck that. Do better.'

'All right. It's coming to you in a will. Clean as a whistle. Nothing to launder, nothing to lie about. No questions asked. Legal and absolutely above board.'

Paul whistled. 'Whatever's going on, it sounds like some truly exceptional kind of fuck-up.'

'You've got no idea, mate. Seriously.'

'Are you okay?'

'Do you care?'

'Of course I do. I don't like all this business any more than you do. Discussing money with friends makes me feel queasy.'

'Then you're in the wrong business.'

He thought about it and said: ‘If you’d have pointed that out twenty years ago, we’d all be in a happier place this morning.’

‘I think I did point it out.’

‘I didn’t listen. I’m a cock. Do you fancy a drink?’

‘If you’re buying.’

‘I’ll buy. If you can lend me twenty pounds.’

‘Are things that bad?’

‘They’ll get better. As soon as I’m part of the property-owning democracy.’

‘All right. Then I’m buying. Assuming this conversation is over.’

‘I hope so. It’s given me a headache.’

They went to the pub.

41

Becks took the call at work. She was having a tough day, trying to deal with the fallout from another budget holiday firm going bust. Thousands of customers stuck in Greece and Spain and the Canary Islands and everyone clamouring at Becks as though it were her fault.

So at first the call from the police did nothing but irritate her — after days and days of hearing nothing, suddenly they wanted her at the station without delay. Then the irritation dropped from under her feet like a false floor and in her normal voice, not her work voice, she said: 'What is it?'

Officer Jenny Cates said, 'If you could come in as soon as possible, that would be great. We'll send a car if you like.'

Becks was there in forty-five minutes.

Jenny Cates showed her the cassette tape that had arrived in the post that morning — postmarked Yate, two days previously.

Jenny Cates said, 'I have to ask you, did you send this tape?'

'Why would I send you a tape? I don't think I've even seen a cassette tape since I was, like, eleven.'

‘We believe that tape may have been made by Jonathan.’

‘By Jonathan? Why?’

‘I’m afraid I can’t go into that. I’d like to you listen to a little bit of it and tell me if you think it’s Jonathan’s voice. Can you do that?’

‘I can do that, yes. Why?’

Jenny pressed Play.

Becks heard:

My name is Jonathan Reese. I am making this recording of my own free will and without coercion.

Jenny pressed Stop. ‘Is that Jonathan’s voice?’

‘What else does he say?’

‘So you confirm that it’s Jonathan Reese’s voice on the tape?’

‘Yes, that’s him. What else does he say?’

‘You’re absolutely sure?’

‘I know his voice. What else does he say?’

‘I’m afraid that’s sensitive to an ongoing investigation.’

‘Please.’

‘Rebecca, I’m sorry, I can’t go into further detail.’

‘Is it a confession?’

‘I can’t confirm or deny the further contents of this recording.’

'It's a confession. Oh my God.' Becks had a feeling. Something was rushing through her, powerful and cold. 'Does he say he did it? Is that what he says?'

'Rebecca, we're concerned by the timing of this tape's arrival.'

'What do you mean?'

'Did you post it?'

'No.'

'Then do you have any idea who might have? Any friends of Jonathan's? Anything like that?'

'No. Why?'

'Because it was posted after Jonathan . . . '

'After Jonathan what?'

'Killed himself.'

'What are you saying to me? Jesus. I don't understand. What are you saying?'

'Is this your handwriting?'

She showed Becks a facsimile of the little handwritten Jiffy bag in which the tape had been posted. In small but scruffy writing, it read: 'URGENT!!! Re: Jonathan Reese.'

'That's not my handwriting. You know my handwriting. You've seen it on forms.'

'Are you at all familiar with this handwriting?'

'No.'

'You're sure.'

'Absolutely.'

'Okay. Thank you for coming at such short

notice. We wouldn't have asked if it wasn't important. Will you be okay? I know this is upsetting and I'm sorry. Would you like me to call someone to take you home?'

'No. Yes. Can you call Ollie?'

'Oliver Quinlan?'

'Yes. I don't think I can call him. I don't think I can speak.'

'We can do that. Do you mind waiting here? Just for a moment?'

'No. No, that's fine. I'll wait.'

Jenny left the room with appropriate deference and respect. But she gathered pace and by the time she got to the office, she was practically running. Everyone looked up.

Jenny took a breath, enjoying the moment. She said: 'The girlfriend confirms. It's him.'

* * *

When the fuss had died down a bit, they got on the phones, getting paperwork done, negotiating with civilian contractors.

Jenny sat at her desk. She had a pair of headphones jacked into her yellowing old PC. She pressed the space bar and listened again to the digital copy of the analogue tape that had arrived that morning.

My name is Jonathan Reese. I am making this recording of my own free will and without coercion. I wish to confess that on June 27th, 2004 I killed my wife Caroline Reese after a drunken argument. I punched her; then suffocated her with a cushion. I took her body to the deserted Hazel farm near the Bath Valley Woods . . .

Ollie came to the police station to pick Becks up.

Outside, next to his dirty van white in the bright sunny drizzle, he said: 'Are you okay?'

Becks frowned, not quite there. 'Yeah. Yeah, I'm fine.'

She looked pale and bewildered. Ollie thought it might be shock. He said, 'Should I call your work?'

She stopped walking in circles and clutched her jacket in her fist. 'Would you mind?'

He dug out his phone and she dictated the number. Ollie turned his back on her to make the call, then hung up. 'All done.'

'What did you say?'

' 'Personal problems'.'

She laughed and ran her hands through her hair. 'Shit.'

'So what do you want to do?'

'I don't know.'

'What did he say? On the tape. What did he say?'

'I don't know. That he did it, I suppose. Why else send it?'

Ollie thrust his hands in his pockets and looked at the sky.

Becks said, 'I'm sorry.'

'Who sent the tape?'

'They don't know.'

'Was it Jonathan?'

'They don't seem to think so. They showed me the envelope, the handwriting. To see if I recognized it.'

'Did you?'

'No.'

'Christ. I need to sit down.'

He didn't even make it into the van, just sat down with his back to it and took off his beanie and worried it around in his hands.

Becks sat down next to him.

He said, 'What do we tell his mum and dad?'

'I don't know. I expect the police will tell them.'

'Do you think?'

She shrugged. 'I don't know. Maybe not.'

* * *

Ollie got into the van to make the call.

When he got back in, he told her that Dennis had been shocked and polite — it was funny, how they were all suddenly being so polite to each other. He'd thanked Ollie for letting him know.

Ollie had told Dennis he'd be in contact. He told him to look after himself and his wife. Dennis said he'd call the police to see if there was any further news.

Then Ollie had hung up.

Becks was in the seat next to him, just looking at the traffic and the people. She said, 'Can you take the day off?'

'I reckon, yeah.'

'Then let's go to your place and get drunk.'

* * *

It was a small, dingy flat in a Victorian block, not far from Jonathan's house. The kitchen was a mess and on the walls were posters of bands Becks had never heard of: Hawkwind, King Crimson, Chrome.

The shelves were lengths of timber propped on house bricks. Along them were many hundreds of vinyl LPs, more vinyl than Becks had ever seen.

There were no curtains, just some Indian cloth pinned above the windows. The air in there was pale orange like a half-sucked sweet.

They started on a bottle of Bulgarian wine from the corner shop and talked about Jonathan — how they'd met him, what a laugh he was, how considerate, how he allowed himself to get comically stressed by the small things, but how you'd always want him by your side in a crisis.

They opened a second bottle. Ollie rolled a joint. Nothing too strong, just taking them down to where they needed to be.

Ollie asked Becks if — deep down — she'd ever thought he might have done it.

Becks said, 'Why? Did you?' and began to cry. She told him she felt dirty, like she needed a bath.

Ollie held her hands. 'Don't be silly. You're lovely. It's me who should've known. It's me.'

And she told him, 'Don't be silly.'

It wasn't his fault. He'd been a good friend.

Ollie looked so sad, with his big eyes and his dirty nails. And then she was kissing him, slipping her tongue into his mouth. And Ollie placed his hand on her leg under her work skirt; then less cautiously, higher up her thigh. She wriggled her hips and then his hand slipped higher. The first time, it was urgent and hurt and angry. The second time it was slower and better.

Becks lay naked in Ollie's grey-white sheets and later they sobered up but didn't dress. They just sat naked, watching the TV, waiting for the news.

42

Kenny was less worried about leaving the cottage, these days. Jonathan was too weak and demoralized to attempt another escape.

So Kenny decided to catch the bus into town. He felt too tired to drive.

He met Pat outside his solicitor's office. She gave him Paul Sugar's details, handwritten on a page ripped from her pocket diary.

Kenny read the page, tried to memorize the details, failed.

* * *

The solicitor was called Desmond Cale. Kenny had known him long enough to watch him get cherubically fat, then divorced, then bald and thin, then remarried and fat again.

In Cale's office, Kenny described the codicil he wanted to add to his existing will.

Cale asked no questions, not even when Kenny referred to Pat's note in order to recite Paul Sugar's details.

Then the business was done. Kenny said goodbye to his solicitor, shaking hands.

Outside, he handed Pat an envelope. It

contained a copy of the amended will. Pat took the envelope and put it in her handbag.

Kenny said, 'Jonathan Reese killed her. He told me.'

'Like I give a shit.'

Kenny wanted to say something else, but he didn't know what.

Pat walked away. He couldn't watch. It made him miss her acutely, as if he were dead already.

He wanted to run after her, stop her, grab her elbow, gabble out what he'd done: that he'd reached into the void and dragged Callie Barton back into the light, made her a story with an end.

But he couldn't do it, not without explaining that Jonathan Reese was still alive, bound, beaten and half-starved in the last bedroom.

He walked to the bus-stop with his hands in his pockets. He took the long ride back home, listening to people being polite to one another. He watched them get on the bus and then get off the bus, thanking the driver —

Cheers, driver, they said.

He missed them all. He missed everyone.

43

Paul Sugar sat at home, plonked his laptop on the coffee table and leaned over it, checking out the websites of local estate agents, making notes on a reporter's pad.

£249,995
GREY COTTAGE, LANGPORT ROAD

A four bedroom mid-terrace cottage built of local natural stone within walking distance of the town and benefiting from a large rear garden.

£310,000
TAUNTON ROAD

A grade II listed period property of great importance being linked with the Abbey of Glastonbury and possibly dating from the sixteenth century.

He knew neither of these was his cottage, because it wasn't even on the market — but going through the listings was like scanning porn while anticipating sex.

About five thirty, the doorbell rang.

Paul shuffled to the door and opened it.

There stood Ashley and Glen: collection boys for Edward Burrell the Shylock.

Paul was a big man, but he stood eclipsed in their monolithic shadow. They were bouncers, doormen bulked up with power-lifting and steroids.

Paul said, 'It's only Thursday.'

'We're busy,' said Ashley. Apparently, he had an IQ of 150. Paul had yet to see much evidence of this.

Glen closed the door and put it on the latch — the chain like a filigree necklace between his sausage fingers.

Paul backed away, saying: 'Actually, I've got some good news on the money front.'

Ashley gripped Paul's testicles and gave them a single, pitiless twist. Paul curled up, nursing his balls. Ashley stepped on his head.

From under the tread of Ashley's boot, Paul made a noise that didn't sound like a human being had made it. He sounded liked a pig at slaughter.

Then Ashley dragged him to his feet and tossed him into the wall.

The shelves collapsed. All the things that had been on them fell down on Paul's head — books, ashtrays, empty bottles, a framed photo of his mum and dad's wedding.

Ashley removed his broad leather belt, wound it round his fist and began to flog Paul with the buckle.

When he stopped, Paul was curled up and sobbing on the floor.

Ashley said, 'Get up.'

Paul got up.

'Sit down.'

Paul sat down.

'So. What's this good news?'

'That I've come into some money.' He couldn't speak properly. He'd bitten a good chunk out of his tongue.

'So where is it?'

'Come on. You just gave me the beating. That must get me another week.'

'That wasn't a beating. That was just saying hello.'

'Okay. Look, it's complicated.'

'Then explain it slowly.'

'I've come into a property.'

'What property?'

'That's the thing. I don't actually know what property. Not exactly.'

Ashley's brow knit.

Paul said, 'It's complicated, but it's kosher. On my life. On my mother's life. I can pay it back. The whole lot.'

'When?'

'Soon. Really, really soon. On my dad's life.

On my little boy's life.'

'You got a little boy?'

'He lives with his mum.'

'Of course he does. What's his name?'

Paul didn't want to say his name. He just said, 'On his life. I promise. I absolutely promise.'

Ashley deliberated for a moment, then ambled over and sat next to Paul. The sofa complained. Two big men, side by side like old women at a bus-stop.

Ashley grabbed Paul's ear and tugged it.

Paul struggled.

Glen put down the magazine he was reading and strolled over. He gripped Paul's ankles.

Soon, Paul was lying face-up in Ashley's lap, thrashing like a landed shark.

Glen leaned over and chopped at Paul's diaphragm with the edge of his hand. Paul tried to gasp, but couldn't. No air would come in.

Ashley pinched Paul's nostrils shut and pressed his other hand flat across Paul's mouth.

Paul tried to breathe, to yell for help, to plead. He tried to twist and jerk his way free.

But not for long.

* * *

When he awoke, he was in the bath. He opened his eyes and sat up. Ashley and Glen had let themselves out.

Before leaving, they'd amputated the little finger of his left hand. They'd burned the stump to cauterize it.

Paul cupped the mutilated hand to his armpit and wailed with pain and shame.

In another world, another time, his sobbing might have driven one of his neighbours to call the police. But nobody called the police and nobody came to help.

Eventually, he lumbered to the kitchen, looking for whisky. Then he called his ex-wife to ask for money.

He said, 'They cut off my finger!'

She said, 'Drop dead, Paul. Really,' and hung up.

Paul finished the litre of whisky.

* * *

In the morning, he sat shuddering on the toilet. The stump of his finger throbbed percussively. He could hear it, the drumbeat of his mutilation. He felt more wretched than seemed possible.

From the bottom drawer in the kitchen, under a pile of old tax returns, he dug out a blister pack of Dexedrine — doing his job, sometimes it was necessary to stay awake for long periods.

He popped three of the little pills and drank a can of Red Bull, then gagged and spent some time coughing and retching.

He shambled to the bathroom and stood under a cold shower. He yelled. He couldn't stand it. It was painful. Then it wasn't painful any more, and he was awake and alert.

He washed himself, one handed. He washed his great barrel chest and his immoderate belly and his mastiff head. Then he padded, hairy and dripping, to the kitchen. He snipped away the swollen, wet bandage on his left hand. The stump looked like a hot dog with mayonnaise and ketchup.

He dabbed the stump with antiseptic — the smell of a childhood spent on another planet — then strapped two fingers together using tape. It hurt like a bastard. He started to cry. Then he took a big, brave sniff and stopped.

The amphetamines were kicking in. Paul's head was darting and dashing with multiple thoughts, impressions, ideas.

He had an idea. It was a good idea. The more he thought about it, the better it got.

He took four more of the humble little pills, wondering why he didn't take them more often — what was the point of not taking them, when they gave you so many good ideas?

He cleaned his teeth and drank some chocolate milk to chase off the nausea. Then he got dressed — navy blue suit, black polo shirt, suede shoes with rubber soles. His hand was awkward, as if he was wearing a boxing glove. But it hardly hurt at all; it only hurt when he remembered it.

He got his car keys and his threadbare wallet and trudged out of the door.

His head was a great ship's engine, gears and pistons and fire. And for once the sun was out. It was a sunny day, it was Friday, and Paul Sugar needed money very, very badly.

44

Kenny checked on Jonathan as he would a sick relative. He found him sitting silently, head bowed and eyes wide in his gaunt face, shining white in the murk.

Kenny said, 'Almost over', and closed and locked the door.

He sat in the living room and turned on the TV. But he was restless; there was an itch in his hands and the back of his neck. He went to the computer and printed off a map of Bath Valley Woods.

When he couldn't stand it any longer, he drove the Combi to the A63 and along some B roads, then parked it in a deserted picnic area. He walked, trudging through long grass and wild garlic, hands buried in the pockets of his kagoul, taking them out now and again to refer to the map.

He was accompanied by the desolate barking of crows. He stopped in a copse of hazel and oak, looking down across the patchwork of the countryside. He was looking at the south-eastern edge of the Bath Valley Woods, at the skeletal remains of a farmhouse.

Far below was the police search team. A large white tent, which Kenny supposed had been erected over the ancient cesspit in which her remains lay. People ducked their heads as they came and went through the entry flap.

There were Land Rovers with flashing blue lights, men and women in white paper jumpsuits; two of them with video cameras, one with an SLR. Yellow digging equipment idled at the edge of the operation, men in work-boots, hi-vis tabards and hard-hats smoking roll-ups, not talking much.

Kenny patted his pockets and lit a cigarette, his first for years and years.

He thought it would nauseate him, but it didn't; he felt the smoke draw through his lungs and into his veins and rise to his brain. It clarified his vision.

He sat with his back to a tree, smoking, watching them far below.

He stayed through a storm of rain that soaked him to the bone; he stayed while the gaggle of journalists, behind traffic barriers, grew bored and shit-kicking. He was still there when the portable arc lights were erected and turned on.

The journalists drifted off one by one. The rain went away and came back again. The sun came up and the mist rose pale grey from the green earth.

The arc lights went off, and the police began to disassemble the tents and put them into the back of trucks.

He watched the weary and dejected police officers have one more coffee and maybe a cigarette, then pack up and go home.

* * *

Wherever Callie Barton was, she wasn't here. She wasn't in the cesspit where Jonathan had said she'd be.

Kenny stood up, smoking another cigarette. He was shivering.

He walked back to the Combi, the grass soaking him to the knees. He could hear his breathing. A plane went by overhead.

He wondered what he would do now.

45

Kenny stood in the semi-darkness of the last bedroom, arms folded, watching.

Jonathan said nothing. His hair was greasy, his clothes were filthy and he reeked of piss and shit. Kenny hadn't really noticed the smell until now.

He was very tired. The long night in the rain had enervated him. He wondered what he must look like, steaming damp and defeated.

He said, 'You didn't do it.'

Jonathan was looking at him, vigilant but calm. 'No.'

'Then why say you did?'

'Because you'd have killed me if I didn't.'

Kenny couldn't reply to that. He swayed like a tree, thinking. Then he said, 'What happened? What really happened?'

Jonathan pointed to his throat. He said, 'My throat hurts. I'm thirsty.'

'I'll get you some water.'

'No. Look at me. Look at me.'

But Kenny had already seen him. He'd seen him when he walked through the door. He'd seen the emaciated creature he'd made.

Kenny went to the window and pulled down the thick curtain he'd pinned there. Thin sunlight, the colour of barley, stabbed through the many chinks in the wood. He recalled what it had been like to be trapped in Jonathan's attic — to go through Callie Barton's belongings, her private, forsaken things. Her footprints in her shoes.

He'd looked for her in boxes and found nothing. He'd seen her face on the internet. He'd seen her being penetrated. And yet he knew nothing about her, not a single thing — except that she had once, a long time ago, been a little girl who was nice to him.

The streaks of sunlight fell on Jonathan and made him a burned effigy, with his black, bruised limbs and his crusted blood and his dry lips and his bright white eyes. And yet he'd clung to life. He was still alive.

Kenny said, 'I'm sorry.'

46

Pat opened the caravan door and knew that something was wrong. Paul Sugar's eyes had a strained gleam and there was a fat bandage round his left hand. It was leaking something the colour of nicotine.

She said, 'Paul!'

Paul grinned. Then the grin fell away and he stepped into the caravan with his customary delicacy, ducking his massive head. The cats made room for him.

Pat said, 'Brew?'

'Lovely.'

She filled the kettle from the tap. 'So what happened to the hand?'

'Someone cut off my finger.'

Pat knew from the dead sound of his voice that she was in trouble.

She glanced at the door. There was no way she could get there before he did — even if she could, there was no way she'd get to her car before he caught her.

She weighed the kettle in her hand. If she swung it with enough force . . .

But if she wasn't fast enough or strong enough, that would be the end of it. So she put the kettle on to boil and got some cups from the cupboard, saying, 'Who did it?'

'Debt collector.'

'You owed him a finger?'

'It was a down-payment on a pound of flesh.'

She laughed. Paul stood there, twitching on the edge of her vision.

He said, 'Pat, I need to borrow some money.'

'I've done what I can with the money, love.'

'Not all the money. Some of the money. Not very much. But I need it today.'

'How much?'

'A couple of grand. Two and a half, if you could make that. Just a loan. Three grand. Five grand would be perfect.'

'What am I, made of it?'

He was having trouble controlling his hands. 'I really, really need it.'

'I'm sorry, old son.'

'I need it.'

'Go to the bank.'

'I went to the bank.'

'Paul . . . '

'Your friend. The man with the cottage. He can give me some money.'

'He hasn't got any money.'

'Come on! He must have a car to sell. A flat-screen TV. He must have something. He can get his hands on two grand. All I want, all I need is a couple of grand.'

'He's got nothing. Just the house.'

'He's got his freedom.'

'He's dying.'

'We're all dying. I need the money.'

'Paul, I'd love to help. Honestly.'

'I don't even want to know who he is. Just pick up the phone. I'll wait in the garden. I'll sit in the car. Give him a call. Two grand! You can raise two grand between you, surely? What's two grand?'

'About a finger's worth?'

Paul picked up the telephone and shoved it into Pat's face. 'Give him a fucking call.'

Pat looked him in the eye. 'No.'

Paul slapped her.

Her face jolted sideways. When it came back, it was wearing a different expression, one that wasn't so big. Paul slapped her again.

Pat glared at him and slapped him back, hard. 'Back off, Paul. And calm down.' But her voice quivered when she said, 'I didn't think you had this in you. Bashing up old ladies these days, is it?'

Paul began to sob. Through the tears, he said, 'Are you going to tell me who this man is and where he lives?'

'No. I can't do that.'

'Please, Pat.'

'No.'

'I'm begging you. Look at me. I'm absolutely begging you.'

'I can't do it. Beg all you want, I can't do it.'

Paul took out his knife and thumbed open the blade. 'Tell me!'

Pat stood very calm and very still. 'I can't. Now put the knife away, sit down and have a cup of tea.'

Paul was still weeping when he stabbed Pat with a punching motion. The blade went in between the second and third ribs on her left side.

She staggered, grasping at the Melamine worktop.

Paul stabbed her again and she collapsed.

He straddled her, pinioned her arms with his knees. He took a breath and moaned in self-pity. Bubbles of snot rose and popped in his nostrils. 'Tell me!'

Pat looked him in the eye.

He said, 'Tell me! Tell me! Tell me!'

But she wouldn't.

He stabbed her again.

Still, she said nothing.

So he stabbed her again. Once he started stabbing, he found it difficult to stop.

★ ★ ★

Paul sat on the floor next to Pat's body and lit a cigarette. His hand was wet and red and sticky. He felt cried-out and drained. Blood soaked the filter-tip.

But he couldn't sit still. He knew no one was coming, and he knew no one had seen what had happened here. But his car was parked outside, with its number plate displaying itself to all the world.

What he had to do was search the caravan. It wouldn't take long; if there was one thing Paul knew, it was how to search a place. He knew there'd be something to identify the man who owned the cottage — even if it was just a number programmed into Pat's mobile.

In less than a minute, he found a copy of Kenny's will in Pat's handbag. It couldn't have been easier.

He was disgusted at Pat, revolted by the meaninglessness of the death she'd allowed herself to die. He felt let down, betrayed and angry.

He pocketed the will, then opened one of Pat's litre bottles of gin. He took a swig before glugging gin round the caravan; plenty of it — especially in the kitchen. Then he turned on all three gas burners. They were attached to a liquid butane cylinder housed beneath the caravan.

On top of the gas burners, Paul spread a

copy of the *Bristol Evening Post*.

The papers began to burn; red-black ashes flitting like fairies round and round under the low ceiling.

By the time he got to his car, the caravan was burning fiercely. Paul didn't know why, but he thought of a Viking boat.

He watched it burn in the rear-view mirror as he drove away, a mushroom of smoke growing thin as it merged with the sky. Soon the flames would reach the butane gas bottle and the field would shine for a moment, bright as the surface of the sun.

47

Kenny sat in the armchair and didn't move. He looked at the wall. He didn't see anything projected on it; it was just a wall. It glowed bright as the sun hit it. Then it faded a little.

He went to the kitchen and took a little vegetable knife from the drawer. He'd picked up four of them for a couple of quid each one day in Weston. It had a red plastic handle.

He walked down the hall, to the last bedroom.

* * *

Seeing Kenny with the knife, Jonathan flinched and cowered.

Kenny lay a palm on Jonathan's head. He left it there, as if in benediction.

Then he squatted and cut Jonathan's hands free.

It was hard going. The flesh round the cable ties had swollen; Kenny had to work the tip of the knife in and under. When Jonathan's hands were free, Kenny cut the cable ties that bound his feet to the chair.

Then Kenny dropped the knife and went to sit with his back to the wall, his hands dangling between his knees.

It would have been nice if Jonathan had just stood and dusted himself down, collecting his dignity, then walked away, closing the door behind him.

But Jonathan was too weak and parched and hurt. The circulation returning to his hands and feet made him writhe and cry out.

Kenny made himself sit there, listening and watching. He made himself memorize what he saw on Jonathan's face — he never wanted to forget, not in the time he had left.

At length, Jonathan dragged himself across the room and sat opposite Kenny. They faced each other across the bare floorboards.

Some time passed.

Jonathan opened his mouth, about to say something. But Kenny shook his head. It didn't matter.

Jonathan nodded.

Kenny felt close to him. In that moment, he loved him.

He watched Jonathan struggle to his feet and sway, reaching out to the cool wall. He watched him shuffle towards the door.

He took the door handle and turned it. There was no sense of occasion; it was just a door handle being turned, and beyond it was just a hallway.

Jonathan blinked in the brighter light.

Then there was an urgent hammering at the door.

48

Kenny stopped Jonathan leaving. He took his elbow, whispering, 'Stay there.'

He left Jonathan in the last bedroom and padded to the front door on feet that felt very light.

He opened the door to a very large, balding man whose left hand was mummified in a dirty bandage and who had a fine spray of what looked like blood across his massive brow.

'Kenny Drummond?'

'Yes.'

'May I come in?'

Kenny looked up at him and felt very small. 'I'm afraid it's not really convenient.'

'My name is Paul Sugar. I'm a friend of Pat Maxwell's.'

'Oh. Right. You're the one who's getting the house.'

'That's right. So may I come in?'

'I'm sorry to be rude, but not really.'

'Well, I'm afraid I need to come in. I really do.'

Paul loomed over him. There was an inevitability about him.

Kenny said, 'All right', and stood aside.

Paul came into the cottage, ducking his head. He trailed something in with him. Kenny didn't know what it was.

Paul was glancing round. It was the natural response of a curious new owner entering a house for the first time — but Kenny knew that Paul wasn't just glancing; he was assessing, recording, checking out entries and exits.

The house was quiet. Kenny could sense Jonathan, soft as a cat in the last bedroom.

So he led Paul through to the studio. They stood under the pollen-filmed glass ceiling; it softened the light and gave the room a kind of nostalgia.

Paul looked around, appreciating what he saw. Kenny had his hands in his pockets, to keep from wringing them. He said, 'What did Pat tell you?'

'Less than you might think. She's a good friend to you, bless her. She's got a good heart.'

'I know.'

'So, the thing is, Kenny — I need money.'

'Sorry?'

'I need two thousand pounds today. Five would be better. The rest of it, I can wait for. For a little bit.'

'I haven't got two thousand pounds. I

haven't got any money. Do I look like I've got money?'

'Sell a painting.'

'Ha!'

Kenny looked at the paintings stacked against the walls, on the easels. Paul's presence had damaged them like light damaged a negative.

Paul said, 'I'm embarrassed. I wish I could say never mind, and go home. But you see this?' He raised his damaged hand. 'Next time, they'll do worse.'

'Who?'

'People. So I'm sorry. But I'm not going anywhere until you've given me some money.'

Kenny ran his tongue over his teeth.

Paul said, 'We both know, you and me — when a man's in above his head, that's when he's going to surprise himself, that's when he's going to see what he's capable of. And I'm desperate, Kenny. I'm in way, way above my head.'

Kenny felt child-sized and fragile in this man's presence. 'I haven't got the money. My bank account's overdrawn. There's the VW, I could sell that if you wanted. But you'd need to clean it up, and you won't get more than a couple of hundred for it. It's a classic, but nobody's buying anything. There's a downturn.'

'Isn't there just.'

'Did Pat send you here? Did she tell you I had money?'

'No. I told you. She's a good friend to you.'

Kenny looked at the spray of blood on Paul's brow.

Paul said, 'Okay, so here's what I'm going to do now. I'm going to call the police. And I'm going to tell them what you did.'

'I didn't do anything.'

Paul looked at Kenny and grinned. Then he reached into his pocket and took out a mobile phone. It looked comically small in his hand.

Kenny thought of Mary and Stever. He watched Paul Sugar, this man with his blood-flecked brow and his bright blue eyes.

He said, 'Do what you want; call the police. It means you don't get the cottage. This place is worth a lot more than two thousand pounds.'

'Not if I don't get two thousands pounds today, it's not. Money's no good if you're not around to spend it.'

Kenny took his hands from his pockets, shrugged. 'If I can't do it, I can't do it.'

Paul crossed his massive arms and planted his feet wide. He tilted his head with a physician's concern. 'How long have you got left?'

'I don't know. A week or two.'

Paul made a remorseful face. 'That's much too long for my purposes.'

He flexed the fingers of his good hand. Then he stepped forward, grabbed Kenny and tucked him into a headlock.

Kenny kicked out. Things fell over: easels and jars and stacked paintings. Kenny clawed at Paul's skin, grabbed at his clothes.

Paul tightened his elbow and Kenny's field of vision began to redden, black at the edges. He clawed and scratched at that freckled, butcher's forearm.

He could feel his fingers weakening, far away. His legs gave way beneath him, skidding around like a baby giraffe.

Paul knelt, taking Kenny's weight as he collapsed, keeping him in the armlock, tightening it.

Kenny could smell Paul's musty clothes, the pus and antiseptic of his bandaged hand.

Paul squeezed harder, grunting.

Kenny's vision shrank towards a radiant terminal point.

49

Paul held on for a few seconds, making sure Kenny was fully unconscious. Then he stood, working through his options.

He searched the studio. Eventually, he found a ball of hairy string and used it to hog-tie Kenny; thumb-to-thumb and wrist to ankle.

He went to the kitchen, opening cupboards and cabinets with great awkwardness, using his elbows and feet to avoid leaving fingerprints.

In the cupboard under the sink he found a pair of Marigold gloves. He slipped one onto his good hand, using his teeth to finish the job.

Then he looked round Kenny's room, feeling under the mattress, rummaging in the wardrobe, exploring the bookshelves. He wasn't looking for anything in particular, not even money. Searching just helped him to think.

Then he found the bathroom and went inside. He opened the medicine cabinet and saw Kenny's painkillers.

Paul took the bottle from the medicine

cabinet. He shook it. It made a dry, whispery, percussive sound that reminded him of primary school.

He left the bathroom, still thinking. The pills weren't right. Paul didn't even know if he could open the child-proof bottle using his one good hand.

He returned to Kenny's wardrobe and opened it. He pushed the clothes to one end. There was only one necktie in there, a vivid purple paisley.

Paul began to knot one end of the tie, using his teeth. When he'd done that, he tested the heft and strength of the door knob.

He returned to where Kenny lay. He stooped, took a big breath, then grabbed Kenny by the collar and dragged him across the studio, through the kitchen, to the bedroom.

He took a break. His lower back hurt. Then he knelt, licking his lips with a quick tongue, and looped the necktie round Kenny's throat.

He lifted Kenny, bundling him up, so that the other end of the necktie would reach the door handle. He began to tie the knot.

Then he heard a noise.

⋆ ⋆ ⋆

It had come from down the corridor, from a room at the dim end of the long hallway.

Probably, it was a cat. A dog would have barked.

Paul let Kenny go and straightened, taking a few moments to replay the last minutes in his mind. He realized that if someone was hiding in the room, they'd heard Kenny use his name.

He listened, breathing hard. Then he crept up to the closed door of the last bedroom. It radiated a fearful silence.

He opened the door and stepped inside.

There was something wrong with the room. For a second, Paul thought it was the smell — like drains gone bad.

Then he noticed the timber fastened to the external window-frame, the radiator that had been ripped from the wall, an inch of amputated copper piping jutting from it. He noticed the upended kitchen chair with ribbons of duct tape attached to it. And he noticed the filthy, ragged man standing — crouching really — in the far corner.

Paul and the ragged man faced each other in silence. The room was full of their breathing.

At great length, Paul said, 'Jesus Christ. Are you Jonathan Reese?'

The man didn't speak. He just crouched there, watching Paul through white eyes.

Paul said, 'What's happening here?'

The ragged man's voice was a thirsty whisper. Paul had to strain to listen. He was saying: 'Are you the police?'

Paul felt a flash of merriment — not for Jonathan Reese, but at his own expense, for the clusterfuck that was currently his life.

He sized Jonathan up. He was in a bad way, swaying like a sapling.

Paul trod a cautious step closer. Just putting on the right expression made him feel compassion in his heart. Tears shone in his bright blue eyes, glinting in his big, hangdog face. 'Jonathan?'

The ragged man stared at him.

Paul said, 'I'm here for you. Your family sent me to find you. I'm here to take you home.'

The man was thin and blackened as if by soot.

Paul held out a tentative hand. It was still wearing the Marigold glove. 'My name is Paul. I'm not a police officer. But I'm here to help.'

He stood a few feet away, keeping his voice low and sedative. 'I know you're scared. But the man who did this to you is unconscious and secured. The emergency services are on their way. You're safe.'

The ragged man took a shambling step forward. He was crying — estuaries gleaming on his blackened face.

Paul kept the tender little smile on his face, the tears in his eyes, the compassion in his heart.

The man halted before him, cautious as a feral cat.

Paul lay a hand, light but firm, on the man's shoulder. It was a father's gesture, a coach's.

'Jonathan?'

The man tensed, as if about to be struck. 'Yes.'

Paul waited until Jonathan's bunched muscles unknotted under his hand and the strength began to go out of him. He was unmanned by relief.

Then Paul made a vice with his fingers and thumb, digging deep into the muscle beneath Jonathan's delicate clavicle.

Jonathan's eyes widened and he made a dry, hissing sound — like fine sand passing through an hourglass. One hand tugged without effect at Paul's broad wrist.

Paul crushed harder.

Jonathan's inky face grew monstrous. He was folding up, his knees giving way beneath him.

Maintaining his grip, Paul side-stepped and got on one knee behind Jonathan. He released Jonathan's clavicle, tightened an elbow round Jonathan's throat. He flexed his bicep.

Paul grunted with effort, brushing Jonathan's ear with his lips.

Jonathan fought, but he was frail; it was just panic, a childish scrambling. Then he raised his left hand. In it was a small serrated kitchen knife with a red handle.

Jonathan used the knife to slash deep across the inside of Paul's thigh, severing the femoral artery.

* * *

Paul wore an ogre's face; spit and teeth and rage and humiliation. He looked at Jonathan with a terrible hatred. His inside leg was gobbeting blood.

He took a weird, lumbering step. His thigh was sopping. The stain widened and thickened. His trousers clung to him. In his astonishment and fear, he was mumbling urgent nonsense — admonishing himself, urging himself to do something. He clutched at his leg with his bandaged hand. Blood infused the dirty grey, made it black.

He trudged on. Big, flat feet. One shoe slurping with blood. He reached for the door. Stumbled and fell.

Paul dragged himself along the floor with

his good hand. Soon he couldn't move any more. He lay there, face down. He was making gobbling noises.

The bandaged hand hammered at the floor, enraged. It left flattened, bloody prints, like a child's thumb painting.

Jonathan waited, doused in Paul Sugar's blood. It shone on his face and in his hair. There were flecks of it on his teeth. He cleaned them with his tongue and spat on the floor.

Eventually, Paul stopped moving.

Jonathan picked up the knife. It had slipped in his hand when he slashed Paul across the thigh. There was a wound across the meat of his palm. He didn't care.

He left his prison and stalked round the cottage, seeing much of it for the first time. He found Kenny hog-tied and helpless with a purple necktie knotted too tight around his throat. Kenny's face was plum purple under white hair.

Jonathan stood over him.

50

Kenny saw the knife and then he saw Jonathan. He didn't speak. It was difficult to breathe.

Jonathan croaked: 'Who the fuck was that?'

Kenny coughed. His throat was sore. It hurt to speak. He spoke in a rasping whisper. 'I don't really know.'

Jonathan nodded, as if that made sense. He leaned on the wall. 'He was going to kill us both.'

Kenny nodded, as much as he could.

Jonathan said: 'Why?'

'For the cottage, I think. I left him the cottage in my will.'

'But you don't know him?'

'It's a long story.'

Jonathan squinted at Kenny as if he were mad. Then he knelt, put the knife to Kenny's eye. 'You don't know anything about me.'

'I know.'

'Or about her.'

'I know.'

'So who the fuck are you? How did you know Caroline?'

'We went to school together. When we were little.'

'How little?'

'Junior school.'

Jonathan cackled. It became a snarl, then a kind of howl. Blood was dripping from his sliced palm on to Kenny's face. Kenny lay awkwardly on his side, his wrists tied to his ankles, unable to draw a lungful of air.

Jonathan pressed the point of the blade to the skin beneath Kenny's eye. It made a pale indentation, pinkish at the edges.

He pressed harder. The tip of the knife slipped a millimetre into Kenny's skin. Jonathan spoke in a low, confiding mutter: 'Do you really want to know what happened?'

Kenny blinked. *Yes*.

Jonathan said, 'What I think she did: she got on a train or a ferry and just never came home. I don't know if she planned it, or if it was spur of the moment. I think that's what she dreamed about, just running away. Whatever.' He laughed to himself, privately. 'She didn't use her passport, so I always supposed she'd stayed in Europe. Maybe she got to Paris or Barcelona somehow. They were her favourite places. Or she said they were. Mostly, I think she liked the idea of them.' He made a growling sound in his throat, like a dog about to bark. 'You might think you loved her, or that you owed her something. But I really did love her. I fucked it up, but I loved her. Look what it got me. And look what it got you.'

Kenny didn't know what to say, except: 'I'm sorry.'

'What's your name?'

'Kenny.'

'Kenny what?'

'Drummond.'

Jonathan ran his tongue over his teeth. 'She never mentioned you. I never heard your name before.'

'No,' said Kenny.

They were quiet for a while.

Jonathan said: 'How long do you have?'

'Not very.'

Jonathan squatted there, thinking.

Then he cut Kenny free. He put his arm round Kenny's shoulder and helped him to his feet.

They limped to the kitchen, supporting each other. Jonathan poured himself a glass of water. He drank it in one, then grabbed the edges of the sink and lowered his head as if about to vomit. He stayed there until it had passed.

Then he poured another glass and gave it to Kenny, who was standing braced by the wall. The rough string had bruised his wrists.

Kenny massaged his raw throat, drank the water.

They stood together, looking out of the window.

Jonathan said, 'Everything that happened here, nobody can know about it. None of it. I can't let that woman ruin my life any more.'

'No,' said Kenny. 'Me neither.'

51

Kenny called Pat, but she didn't answer. Her machine didn't even kick in. The line just rang and rang.

He tried four times.

He made himself busy. He heated some tinned chicken soup. Jonathan sipped a couple of spoonfuls but couldn't keep it down.

Kenny left him to find some strength and went rummaging for everything they would need. Petrol in the red canister, a blue tarpaulin he found bundled up and mildewed in one corner of an outbuilding; the crowbar; a ball pen hammer that wasn't heavy enough. The little fire extinguisher he kept in the back of the Combi.

He drove to the garden centre, leaving Jonathan to gather deadfall and leaves and other garden waste. Kenny limped round the aisles, buying a short-handled sledgehammer, more rolls of duct tape, some gardening gloves, a garden fork and several rolls of heavy-duty garden refuse sacks.

He returned to find that Jonathan had worked hard in the watery sunshine, labouring slowly to erect a broad-based bonfire, piling it with wood from the outbuildings and with smashed-up old furniture.

They entered the cottage together and worked in the last bedroom. They didn't speak, communicating only with glances and gestures and grunts and, once or twice, a kind of bitter laugh.

They emptied Paul Sugar's pockets of car keys, wallet and a blister pack of Dexedrine. Kenny removed the credit cards from the wallet, cut them up with kitchen scissors, put them in a soup bowl and burned them until they were molten and bubbling like caramel.

In the wallet there were no photographs or other personal items.

They knelt to unlace and remove Paul's huge shoes. One was clammy with cooling sweat, the other was sopping full of blood. They cut off Paul's blood-sodden clothes, leaving him in underwear and socks.

They worked together to tie a yellow tow rope around Paul's chest and hauled him through the kitchen and out of the back door, as if dragging a boat to the edge of the water. He left a trail of faecal matter and blood.

They heaved and strained to drag the body on to the bonfire. Some of the structure collapsed beneath his dead weight. They remodelled the pyre around him.

Kenny doused Paul with petrol from the

red canister. Then they piled more wood and kindling around him, even using some scraps of coal from a long-forgotten scuttle. Kenny poured petrol on the kindling, too. On top of all that they lay the clothing and heaps of dried-out summer leaf-fall.

Then Kenny got on his hands and knees with a lighted twist of paper. He lit the bonfire from its base, where there was no petrol. It took some time to get going, even using the fire-lighters. But when the pale flicker finally reached the petrol the fire roared like a living thing, grinning, licking it's chops, softly growling.

As the bonfire smoked and popped, they wordlessly gathered more fuel to feed it. It needed to burn hot, for a long, long time.

Then, as Jonathan limped into the cottage, Kenny jacked up Paul's car, removed the wheels and rolled them into the darkest corner of the furthest outbuilding.

He removed the number plates and threw them in the fast-moving brook, followed by Paul's empty wallet and car keys and shoes.

He rubbed the car's bodywork, massaging it with handfuls of oily dirt, rubbing it down with an old towel. It was like ageing a painting.

From a drawer in the kitchen he took a carrier bag and returned to the car. He cleaned out the glovebox, under the seats and in the boot. He filled the carrier bag with an A–Z, a dog-eared map book, a squeezed-out tube of HC45 cream, an empty spectacles case, some fluffy boiled sweets, old pens and a paperclip.

Then he used a pack of kitchen wipes to clean each surface — paying special attention to the gear stick, the steering wheel, the door handles, the rear-view mirror. He stuffed the used wipes into another, now bulging carrier bag. He knotted the bag and binned it.

He siphoned the petrol from the tank into the red canister. Then he bundled up some newspaper, soaked it in petrol, threw it into the car and tossed in a match. He let it burn for thirty seconds before dousing the flames with the mini-extinguisher.

When it cooled, the car would look like it had been here for ever. He hoped the smell would dissipate soon; it ruined the illusion. He didn't know how to remove the smell. It would have to do.

Kenny went inside.

Jonathan had mopped and scrubbed the floors with extravagant amounts of cold water and biological washing powder. The last bedroom smelled hot and clean, like a laundrette.

* * *

The sun was setting and the pyre glowed red, the smoke pouring into the darkening sky. Kenny and Jonathan winced in its wavering heat. They threw on more armfuls of leaves. The hair on their arms and their eyelashes singed.

They stepped forward and fed the sketches of Jonathan to the fire, one by one. The chronicle of Jonathan's transformation was received by the flames: paper curled and blackened; moth-light ashes described a slow wandering spiral, circling in the coiling air, glowing briefly red at the edges, bright against smoke that was black with Paul's heat-rendered fat. It was sad and beautiful. It smelled of autumn, of barbecues and burning leaves and the passing of the summer.

Then Kenny and Jonathan sat at the border of endurance, watching it. The flames licked on the shadowed planes of their faces and made them pagan and unfamiliar.

Kenny called Pat, but there was still no answer.

He and Jonathan slept curled up on the hardened, oil-poisoned soil. They woke every half hour and carried more wood to the bonfire, stoking it, keeping it hot. Then they lay down and curled back up and went to sleep.

At dawn it began to drizzle and the remains of the fire, still cracking and popping, began to hiss. They woke to see its charcoal and ashes, the dead branches and blackened earth. In its centre, the darkened skull of Paul had burst. Fragments of jaw and teeth, a shattered grin. Ulna, shoulder blade. Feet on incomplete legs.

Kenny doused the bonfire with water from the blue bucket. It hissed and steamed in the morning drizzle. Bone fragments cracked.

Not far from the cooling bonfire, Kenny lay out a blue tarpaulin, weighing down the edges with carburettors and hand-sized rocks. Then he used the new garden fork and the gardening gloves to drag the burned bones from the bonfire on to the tarpaulin.

He gathered the fragments of skull and jawbone. With needle-tip pliers, he separated the teeth from the skull. It took surprising physical force. The bone fragments radiated their baked-in heat through the gardening gloves. Kenny had to keep putting them down. But eventually he stood, rattling the teeth in his gloved hand like dice, and walked to the edge of his land.

He scattered the teeth over the brook. They

plopped one by one like heavy rain into the cold clear water.

He returned to the remains, putting on the plastic goggles he hadn't worn for five years, since the last time he used spray paint. Kneeling, he used the short-handled sledgehammer to shatter the oddments of skull. Then he pulverized the remaining fragments into smaller splinters of bone and blackened meat and tendon. The spine and the hips were hard work. He didn't know that he sniffed and wept as he worked, on his knees, bringing the hammer down. Bone chips cut his brow and his cheek. He was lucky to be wearing the goggles.

He gathered the pieces into a heavy-duty garden sack. When that was done, he used a broom to sweep bone debris to the centre of the tarpaulin, then a dustpan and brush to get the debris into the sack.

While he remembered, he washed the dustpan and brush in the stand pipe outside.

He returned to the tarpaulin and sealed the garden sack. Then he mummified it with duct tape. When that was done, he slipped the refuse sack inside a second refuse sack, sealed it, then slipped it into a third, a fourth.

He was left with a bulky, airtight bundle. He tucked it under his arm and took it into the cottage and down the hall, to the last bedroom.

* * *

Jonathan had used the crowbar to lever up some of the bare floorboards, exposing the grave-smelling crawl-space beneath. When Kenny entered with the bundle Jonathan stood at its edge, waiting.

Without saying a word, Kenny clambered down into the crawlspace and crouched in its chill. Down here, the soil was alive with worms and pale grubs.

Jonathan passed him a trowel and Kenny lowered himself into the darkness.

He waited, crouching under the low floor, until Jonathan had squeezed the package between the gap in the floorboards. Then Kenny slithered to the dark centre of the crawl-space, dragging the package behind him. It wasn't far, but it was awkward and cold and damp, and it took a long time.

He was out of breath when he reached the centre of the darkness beneath his house. The air smelled rich with soil.

On his hands and knees, the damp floorboards an inch or two above his head, Kenny worked with the trowel. He scooped out a shallow grave, one cupful at a time. His back hurt and his arms hurt — his neck hurt worst of all because he was digging on his knees, hunched over himself.

He didn't speak. If he'd heard his voice echoing down here, he'd have had to leave this awful place, squirming faster and faster towards the pale oblong of sunlight. He'd never have gathered the courage to come back down.

Kenny rolled the bundle of bones into the hole.

It was too shallow.

His heart was light and fast with exertion and anxiety. He ignored the dirt and the cobwebs in his hair and the pain in his lower back and his cramping thighs, the horrible dank blackness. He dug deeper. His hands sweated in the gardening gloves.

At length, he dragged the package into the hole. Then he used his hands to heap earth upon it, and the flat side of the trowel to compact the earth as well he could.

Then Kenny dragged himself back to the light.

Jonathan squatted, offering a hand to help Kenny out of the hole.

Kenny stood in the last bedroom, bathed in rainy sunlight with cobwebs and grave dirt in his hair, gasping like a fish.

Jonathan told him to go and sit down.

Kenny sat in the doorway as Jonathan replaced the floorboards, nailing them in place. He used a rag to massage shoe polish into the new, ashen splits in the dark aged wood.

And then it was done. Kenny had made someone disappear; created an absence from a presence.

He had made the opposite of a portrait.

* * *

He was spent. He showered, massaging his scalp with trembling hands.

They sat on the sofa and tried to eat. Neither of them could manage it.

On the news, Kenny saw Pat's caravan.

Jonathan said, 'What is it?'

'Nothing,' said Kenny. He saw the fire engines and the police cars and the onlookers and the skeleton of the burned caravan and he remembered how Pat had held his hand as they stood watching the pier burn.

He thought of the spray of blood on Paul Sugar's monolithic brow.

He put down his knife and fork. They made a bright domestic sound in the blue darkness.

He went to the kitchen and washed the plate and the knife and fork under cold running water. Then he dried the plate and put it down on the drainer. Then he wept.

52

Kenny woke Jonathan at 4 a.m.

They walked outside amid the sounds of the placid night; the cool before the warm morning.

Jonathan wore Kenny's baseball cap. He sat in the passenger seat of the Combi.

Kenny drove.

* * *

They stopped five miles outside Bath, at the south-eastern edge of an arable field called Round Hill Tyning. The field's centre, dark against the field of stars, rose in a gentle swell.

Kenny sat there with his arms crossed over the steering wheel, looking at it.

Jonathan said, 'Is this it?'

'This is it.'

Kenny and Jonathan stepped out of the Combi and closed the doors, too loud in the silent morning. They climbed the low fence into the dew-wet field.

They walked for a long time in silence, climbing the hill spur as the sun began to rise.

At the top was the Long Barrow, a Neolithic tomb: a hundred feet long and ten feet high, made of blue flint and local granite. The entrance to the underworld was marked with a fossilized ammonite.

They looked down on the village, half a mile away. They were breathing hard with the short exertion.

Kenny said, 'What will you do?'

Jonathan huddled in the borrowed clothes, too small for him, and said: 'Tell them I don't remember.'

'They won't believe you.'

'They'll have to.'

'Your confession. On tape . . . '

'You beat it out of me. Whoever you were.'

Kenny nodded. 'It won't be easy. Keeping up a lie that big.'

Jonathan said nothing. He just turned, facing Kenny.

Here, on the high hill, looking down at that little village, Kenny felt close to him — as if they were brothers returned from a distant war. They had lost the same thing.

Jonathan said, 'What will you do?'

Kenny shrugged.

And that was it — there was nothing to say. Jonathan began to trudge down the other side of that limestone mound, heading for the village. He looked like the ghost of a tinker.

Kenny watched him until he was halfway down the hill. Then Jonathan turned, looking up at him. He had to call out to be heard, even in the quiet of the morning. He said, 'Did you have a nickname? When you were a kid?'

'Yes,' said Kenny.

'Was it 'Happy'?'

'Yes,' said Kenny. The strength had gone from his legs.

'She said you helped her,' said Jonathan. 'She said you were very little. You were shorter than her, and you smelled funny. She said you were a little gentleman. Those were her words.'

Kenny blinked.

He said, 'Thank you.'

The sun was rising now, over the barrow which was an ancient burial chamber and a kind of womb, too: a womb for the dead. Jonathan walked towards the little village, and Kenny knew he would never see his face again.

* * *

Jonathan came to the wet edge of the field and climbed the wire fence. Through the low morning mist, he limped down a country road, heading for the village of Wellow.

He'd passed the church and the war memorial when he heard an approaching car. Soon, a spectral form came at him like a muscular fish through murky water.

There was a snarl as the unseen driver nudged the accelerator. A silver-grey Audi parted the mist.

The driver, a curly-haired young man in a suit and Windsor knot, saw Jonathan — this raggedy man, wild-eyed, bruised black and shambling.

Jonathan hobbled to the centre of the road, waving his arms above his head and shouting.

The driver hit the brakes. The road was wet. He lost control. The Audi coasted laterally towards Jonathan, whose arms stopped waving when he saw what was happening.

A car skidding. A crazy man with his arms raised, alone on a country road. Behind him the milk white sky and the brown field, some crows, the sunrise.

53

Kenny packed a bag with some trousers, T-shirts, underwear, books, his medication. Then he walked round the cottage one more time. The air was heavy with Paul Sugar's presence and Jonathan Reese's absence.

He locked the windows and the door and slipped the key under the boulder by the wheelie bin. Mary would know it was there.

He tossed his rucksack and one large box into the back of the Combi, then got behind the wheel. He dug in his pocket and pulled out the list. It was balled up and tatty so he flattened it on his lap.

He found a biro in the glovebox and drew a line through Callie Barton's name. So the list read:

Mary
~~Mr Jeganathan~~
~~Thomas Kintry~~
~~Callie Barton~~

Now he saw that the only name remaining uncrossed was the only name that really mattered.

He scrunched up the list and shoved it back into his pocket. It was meaningless, just a piece of paper — but he wanted to dispose of it far from the ground upon which Paul Sugar had trod before vanishing from the world.

He started the engine and drove away.

Desmond Cale agreed to meet him for coffee at 6.30 a.m., so it was still early when he got to Mary's place.

Kenny waited until she opened the curtains and saw the Combi parked outside.

She came to the door, still in her pyjamas.

Kenny got out of the Combi, carrying a taped-up cardboard box. He limped to the open door of the pastel-coloured house on the steep hill.

'Is it too early?'

'Don't be silly,' she said. 'Come in.'

* * *

The kids were eating breakfast. They screamed and set aside their plates when they saw Kenny. Kenny knelt and put down the box, accepting their hugs, the fine smell of them.

When Kenny stood, there was Stever in a pair of stripy pyjama trousers and a washed-out *Futurama* T-shirt.

Kenny and Stever hugged, slapped each other's backs. Stever's beard tickled Kenny's face as he whispered in Kenny's ear, private but unembarrassed: 'We love you, mate.'

When Kenny looked at Mary, she had tears in her eyes. Then she hugged him.

Stever mumbled something about cleaning teeth and getting dressed and ushered the kids from the room.

Mary said, 'You look so tired.'

'I'm okay. I'm fine.'

'Thanks for coming round.'

'I can't stay long.'

'Yes you can. What's this?' She tapped the box with her toe.

'In a minute.' He touched her face, her skin smooth and alive. He said, 'I wanted you to know, I'm leaving the cottage to you and Stever.'

She shook her head, once. 'I don't want to have this conversation.'

'You need to listen to what I'm saying, okay? It's not a holiday cottage. It's in a mess. As soon as it's yours, I want you to take out a little mortgage on it. Not much. Just temporary.'

'Stop saying this. I don't want to hear it.'

'Spend what you borrow from the bank by renovating the place. Get the cars removed from the back yard, get the outbuildings torn down. That'll cost a few thousand. Get the back yard turfed over. Tidy up the hedges at the bottom by the brook and put up a new fence. Inside, it's all right, structurally. You'll need to re-sand the floors, get the place repainted, refit the bathroom a bit, do something to the kitchen. And then you sell it, okay?'

'I really don't want to have this conversation. There's no need for it. Not yet.'

'Yes, there is. I need you to understand. I don't care if you get less than you might have, two years ago. I want it sold and gone. It's not a happy place. It's not a good place.'

'Kenny . . . ' She held his face in both hands and kissed his lips. 'Shhh. Please. Shhhh.'

He disengaged. They looked at each other. He gave her the box.

It was light.

She sniffed and peeled back the tape. Inside the box were the portraits Aled had made of Kenny as a child.

He said, 'I didn't know what else to do with them.'

Mary flicked through pictures of Happy Drummond, this little boy he'd been. Her tears spotted on to the paper, soaked in. They brought the pictures back to life, gave them value.

She sucked a breath through her teeth, wiped at her tears with the heel of a hand, then put down the box and kissed his cheek. 'I love you.'

He smiled and didn't say it. He just felt it, and feeling it made him stronger.

* * *

They crowded in the door to say goodbye — Mary and Stever and Daisy and Otis. They waved and smiled, pretending this parting was not what they all knew it to be, and Kenny drove away.

54

The impact of the car shattered Jonathan's hip and leg and wrist. The paramedics raced him under blues and twos to the Bristol Royal Infirmary, where he lay sedated but conscious, saline and morphine drips feeding into his arm.

The police came to see him, but he couldn't talk. His family came to see him, too. He was aware of them crowding the side of the bed — his mum and dad, Ollie and Becks.

He kept his eyes closed, because he didn't want to talk yet. But even pretending to be unconscious, he could detect a certain stiffness between Becks and Ollie, and he supposed he knew what lay at its core.

He didn't mind. Given the circumstances, it had probably been inevitable.

He wasn't a jealous man, not any more. Once upon a time he had been: he'd paid the price for it.

Jealousy had led him to suffocate Caroline Reese in bed with her pillow, then drag her out of the house in a composting sack and into the back of his van.

The week before, Ollie had given a quote on landscaping the grounds of a mansion refurb just outside Yate. Thinking about this saved Jonathan. He knew that no chain of evidence connected him to that unfinished place; just a couple of calls to Ollie's mobile from the client's mobile, two calls out of hundreds, maybe thousands.

He drove her out there under cover of darkness and buried her in the muddy hollow that soon would become a swimming pool. She was there now, staring up through the soil.

Two years ago, the owner of the mansion had gone bankrupt. Since then, the property had changed hands a couple of times. It always made him feel strange, to think of families swimming in the pool, the shadows of their scissoring legs passing over Caroline's empty eyes.

He'd seen those eyes behind Kenny's, sometimes. She seemed most present in those moments when Kenny went blank — a separate intelligence, staring out through a borrowed face like living eyes in an old portrait. But she was gone now.

Becks took Jonathan's blistered and bandaged hand, kissed his bruised knuckles, brushed her lips along his hairline, whispered in his ear: 'I love you.'

Jonathan heard but didn't speak. He just floated there, half-awake — scared to sleep in case he should dream and mutter aloud the things he knew.

This horror would follow him through the years, a chill undercurrent in the warm new marriage he was about to make with Becks, a woman who loved him, and whom he forgave. But the dread would fade, then it would pass.

Everything does, eventually.

55

Kenny crossed a long bridge and drove all day and much of the night. He parked the Combi in the grassy dunes at the edge of a far beach.

He woke with the sun, chilly and stiff in his bones. He felt clean and good.

He opened the Combi door and stepped into a brisk morning. The sand was rough on the tender soles of his feet.

He cast off his T-shirt and felt the air on him. Then he bolted for the sea. He skipped over green-black tresses of kelp. Here the sand was darker and harder: he left shallow footprints in his wake. They filled with cloudy water and faded away — the marks of his passage on the face of the earth rescinded behind him.

He sprinted into the ocean and cried out at its shocking cold, the brilliant life of it. He raced forward until the foaming water was chest high and seaweed tugged at his ankles like siren hands, caressing and withdrawing.

He ducked his head into the spume and came up soaked and laughing; his white hair in spikes, the salt stinging his eyes.

He took a moment to turn in the water and look back at the Combi — waiting at the edge of the beach with great forbearance, keys dangling in the ignition, a note on the driver's seat.

Then Kenny turned. He aimed west of the sun and east of the moon, and began to swim.

Other titles published by
The House of Ulverscroft:

BURIAL

Neil Cross

Nathan has never been able to forget the worst night of his life: the party that led to the sudden, shocking death of a young woman. Only he and Bob, an untrustworthy old acquaintance, know what really happened and they have resolved to keep it that way. But when, years later, Bob appears at Nathan's door with terrifying news, old wounds are reopened, threatening to tear Nathan's world apart. Because Nathan has his own secrets now. Secrets that could destroy everything he has fought to build. And maybe Bob doesn't realise just how far Nathan will go to protect them . . .